My
Riviera

Books by Sharon Dilworth

The Long White
Women Drinking Benedictine
Year of the Ginkgo

My Riviera

Sharon Dilworth

Carnegie Mellon University Press
Pittsburgh 2018

Many thanks to ever-faithful friends and writers:
Jane Bernstein, Jane McCafferty, Kevin González,
Tim Haggerty, Andrew Sproule, Diane Goodman,
and Jen Bannan. Thanks also to Rissa Ji-Yeon Lee.

Much appreciation to Connie Amoroso and
Cynthia Lamb for their generous help and care on
the production of this novel, and of course forever
gratitude to that tour guide who when I first came
to Pittsburgh, showed me the childhood home of
Dan Marino down in Oakland and told me I might
like it here.

Book design by Connie Amoroso & Rissa Lee

Library of Congress Control Number: 2017949848
ISBN: 978-0-88748-629-6
Copyright © 2018 by Sharon Dilworth
Printed and bound in the United States of America

10 9 8 7 6 5 4 3 2

for Alex, Victor, and Manno

"There is hardly a single action that we perform in that phase which we would not give anything, in later life, to be able to annul. Whereas what we ought to regret is that we no longer *possess* the spontaneity which made us perform them. In later life we look at things in a more practical way, in full conformity with the rest of society, but adolescence is the only period in which we learn anything."

—Marcel Proust, *In Search of Lost Time*

Chapter One

Menton, France 1951

*W*hen I first knew Jules he had two heroes: Henri Matisse, the artist and Fausto Coppi, the cyclist. He explained the contrast between these men as the two sides of his soul but I saw a heart divided.

*M*atisse was eighty-two at the time. Suffering another bout of pneumonia, he spent his days in bed with paper and scissors, working on projects that did not require much physical strength. Rumors concerning his ability to complete the design and decoration of the Chapel in Vence—his showcase of a life dedicated to art and devoted to beauty—were not optimistic. Jules and I worried and waited for news of his further decline.

Jules and I entertained ourselves by exploring the Riviera that spring. He had an enormous black Cadillac and as long as we could find money for petrol, we could go anywhere we wanted. While I preferred the coastal roads, Jules, obsessed with Matisse, usually insisted on Vence.

I was fifteen and living with my older sister Sophie and Grandfather in a family house above the once fashionable, now deadly dull town of Menton. Grandfather was not happy in the south. He complained of the constant sunlight, claiming that it was burning a hole in his skull. He took refuge in his study; a small stuffy room that had previously been used for food storage. It smelled of unpleasant root vegetables—onions, turnips, and rutabagas. The house and the gardens were dull. No one came by, none of us had friends, we never entertained. Life at the villa was punctuated by tirades by Grandfather who thought the end of the world was coming. At least the end of the world as far as France was concerned.

Jules was my only friend on the Riviera. Five years older than me, he was my savior. He took me away from my boring life in Menton and introduced me to another kind of Riviera. With Jules I tried to be witty and interesting; I was constantly thinking of ways to be more intriguing than I was.

"Matisse understands the Riviera better than any other French painter," he lectured. "The light, the sun, the water; he captures it all."

I had left my Parisian school almost a year ago and was still hesitant about offering my opinion on something like art.

What I knew of Matisse, I knew from Jules. I was impressed, but not enamored. I liked what I saw of his work, but for me it did not capture the Mediterranean, not in the way that Jules assured me it did. His paintings were flat. They dulled the visual field with their heavy oil colors and stillness. To me no art could hold the magic of the Riviera. The Riviera moved; nothing there ever stood still. The sunlight shimmered. Having spent my life until that point—fifteen years—in Paris, the Côte d'Azur was another country. Now that I'm older it's unlike anything I'm likely to experience again.

Jules and I could agree on a shared love of the Riviera. We were both awed by the beauty of the region and enamored of the eccentricities of the people who inhabited the coast. We were explorers on a vast playground. Warm, full of sunshine, interesting, exotic people, it was like a treasure chest of things to do and see and I respected Matisse for living and celebrating the area. On the other hand, no one loved it like I did. It was my world, my glorious discovery. I felt I owned it and was not happy about sharing it with anyone, not even Matisse.

Jules could not accept this. "You're right to have your own opinion, but Matisse is Matisse, the greatest artist France has ever produced. You must learn to love him, Agnes."

*J*ules' adoration of Fausto Coppi, the Italian bicycle racer, was much more out of character. Jules was not an athletic-looking man. He wore pressed linen trousers and espadrilles, which he liked to keep clean. He combed back his hair and kept it neat with hair gel. He found tennis boring. "Men and women who spent long afternoons hitting the ball back and forth across a net—deadly," Jules said. And yet, as with Matisse, there was nothing Jules didn't know about Coppi's personal life or his professional career.

"People think of him as a cosmopolitan and savvy, but he's not. He's from a small village in the middle of nowhere just like the rest of us. The son of a local butcher who spent his youth pedaling the streets of Castellania delivering mortadella and salami to the residents of his village."

"Wait a minute," I said and tried to sort out a detail from the multitude of stories Jules had told me about himself. It was always confusing. Sometimes I thought he was talking about himself only to discover he had been telling me about Coppi. "Didn't you tell me *your* father was a butcher?"

"Did I?" Jules asked.

Jules liked to be entertained; even with his own words and truth was not important if the story was interesting. I liked this aspect of his personality and tried to emulate it, but my stories sounded hollow. They most definitely sounded false.

"A butcher in a town outside of Marseille," I said.

"I once worked for a butcher. I delivered meat," Jules said. "All over the city of Marseille. On my bicycle."

"Just like Coppi," I said.

"Do you think?"

"Think what?"

"Think that I'm like Coppi?"

"How would I know?" I asked Jules. "I've never seen the man."

Jules acted as if he was astonished by this revelation. "How can that be? He's been to Paris," Jules said. "In '49, he wore the yellow jersey on the avenue of the Champs-Élysées."

"I didn't see him," I said.

"How could you have missed it? He was in his glory. Yellow jersey, Italian flags everywhere. All the eyes of the world were on him."

"Mine must have been elsewhere," I said. "I would have remembered."

"We cannot go forward with you not knowing," Jules said finally. "We must do something to change that."

And I was happy because that meant another day that we could spend together.

*S*ophie and I had met Jules on the public beach in Monte Carlo, which was one of the reasons Grandfather called him a good-for-nothing.

"He's a short little man with a large motor car, not a thought in his head and as far as I can tell not much more in his wallet," Grandfather judged.

"Jules is not that short," I said. When I thought short, I thought pudgy, which Jules was not. As to what he had in his wallet, I didn't know. He did not always have money, but that didn't seem to bother him. He had no real career ambitions and didn't talk about money like other men. Unsure as to his exact financial situation, I shrugged and repeated what I had already said. "He's not that short."

"But he does parade his idleness in that garish motor car," Grandfather said.

"Garish?" I asked. "It's black."

"But loud."

"It's black," I said. "How can a black car be loud?"

"I'm not talking of the color," Grandfather said. "Black is black. I'm talking about the size."

"It runs perfectly well."

Jules kept it clean with lots of soap and water and he had special soft rags that he used to dry the sides of the car so that the soap did not make streaks. I could not think of anything better than driving the mountain roads of the Côte d'Azur. The Riviera was a splendid place for driving; the roads twisted and climbed. At every turn there was another view of the Mediterranean. The sun shone across the water like a great light caught in diamonds. The salt breeze blew all afternoon and the sun setting off the Dog's Head cliff of Monaco was spectacular.

"The man does nothing but sit in the sun. Have you considered the color of his skin?" Grandfather asked. "It's darker than a coffee bean. Can you imagine him in Paris? He'd be a fish out of water."

"He doesn't live in Paris," I said.

"With good reason," Grandfather said.

"You don't know him," I said.

"I know what I see," Grandfather said.

Grandfather was a fine one to talk about idleness. Grandfather did nothing but pace from room to room in the musty old villa. "This would never have happened in Paris," was his stock reply to everything that happened and upset him. His skin was white, his face so pale it almost had a purplish hue to it. He stayed indoors on even the warmest afternoons.

"He's a grown man," Grandfather said. "What is he doing with himself?" He did not give me time to respond. He had an answer all ready. "Nothing. That's what he's doing. Nothing more than driving around the country. Doing what? Wasting time? Petrol? What does he contribute to humanity?"

I had told Grandfather that Jules worked for a film company in Nice. He scouted out locations and people to be in the director's upcoming film. This was what Jules had told me he was doing when I first met him, though the job didn't seem to keep him busy and I wasn't really sure he was still employed anymore.

Grandfather had too strong an ego—a man continually study-ing his reflection in the glass—though even with so much self-absorption, he found time to bother about everyone else. His interest and displeasure with Jules worried me tremendously. I feared he was going to stop Jules from taking me around the Côte d'Azur.

I waited for my sister Sophie to say something in Jules' defense. Instead she sat on the divan, distracted by something outside the window.

I went over and knocked on her head. "Anyone home up there?" I asked.

Sophie was puzzled by the distraction and pushed my hand away as if she was doing something important. She had washed her hair that morning and had tried to let it dry in the sun. She thought it would lighten it, but the hours in the sun had only made it curly and unruly. We had dark hair like our father. Nothing but age would lighten it.

Grandfather's moods were so mercurial, and I worried that unless we painted a more positive picture of Jules, he would do something rash like lock us up in our rooms until we were twenty-five.

"Say something," I whispered in her ear. She was not one to be quiet when important things were concerned and she was making me furious with her nonchalant attitude.

She was perplexed by my anger; she had not been paying any attention to Grandfather's rants.

"About Jules," I demanded.

"Jules?" Sophie turned from the window and gave a brief moment of attention to the matter at hand. "Jules is great fun."

It wasn't the right thing to say to Grandfather.

He snorted. "What kind of future will you have with a man who is great fun?"

I fumed. Grandfather was not merely pessimistic about the future; he didn't believe there would be one. "Europe is doomed," he mumbled into his brandy snifter. "France is the handkerchief of what was a great man. Now all the empire can do is blow its nose into it. We are nothing." He was less gloomy when he drank but as he worried about his liver, he did not drink as often as I would have liked.

The question was directed at Sophie: Grandfather was not in the habit of caring about my thoughts on things.

"Future?" Sophie said. "I don't plan to have a future with Jules if that's what got you upset. Right now, Agnes and I are being entertained. Agnes is right. He does have a lovely motor car. It's nice to be out. To be seen, to see other people."

She got up from the pillows and went over to where Grandfather stood. She took the brandy glass from his hand and sipped it until it was gone. She handed Grandfather back the empty glass and left the room without another word.

I could not act that way with Grandfather. I had neither the confidence, nor the attitude. I was awkward and scattered around him and did my best not to be alone with him. Sophie had a certain style and elegance. People were struck by her presence. She made an impression.

I mumbled something about checking on Sophie. "She hasn't been feeling all that well."

"She certainly drinks as if she feels well," Grandfather remarked as I chased after my sister.

Sophie was smoking on the patio. Grandfather knew she smoked, but she didn't do it in front of him because he clicked his teeth in disapproval. I started to speak and she hushed me.

"Look," she said and pointed over to the fruit grove where Mathilde, the maid, was struggling to pick lemons. A simple chore, she could take all morning to complete it.

Mathilde was originally from Normandy and had no faith in the warm weather, even after four months on the Riviera. "It's not as it should be," she said and waited for cold or sleet. She wore, just as she had always worn in Paris, a black skirt, a gray and white striped vest. On rainy days she added a white cotton cap. When I teased that she must be warm in such clothes, Mathilde scolded me with misplaced emotions of anger and frustration. "Why do you bother about me? Why do you care what I wear?" She hissed at me like a mad cat. It was fun to laugh at her and Sophie and I spent many hours making fun of her silly ways.

Mathilde's struggles with the fruit trees normally amused me—it made me laugh to see her so annoyed by something as banal and harmless as a tree—but I had other things to think about that day.

"Why didn't you say something in Jules' defense?" I asked Sophie.

"I wasn't aware that Jules needed defending," Sophie said. She flicked the pieces of tobacco from her tongue, but missed the ones on her lips.

"To Grandfather," I said, though I didn't think this was something that needed explaining. "Think of what will happen if he forbids us to go out with Jules?"

"Why do you worry so much?" She came over and cupped her hands under my chin. Her breath smelled of tobacco and brandy, a combination that reminded me of the men's bars in Paris. I pulled away. "You're going to grow old and gray with all this worry."

"Before Jules, I did nothing but stare at the walls of this boring place," I said. "It was awful."

"But nothing's going to ruin our good times," Sophie said. "Grandfather's talk is like the air," she said. "It's there but it never does much damage." Just as she always did, she tossed the end of her cigarette into the thick vines surrounding the bricks of the patio. Were they seeds, she would have her own garden of cigarettes.

"He frets about everything in his life," Sophie said. "He frets that Mathilde doesn't clean the house. He frets that Cook is trying to poison him with bad food. He frets about us and now because we know Jules, he frets about him."

"But none of that is important," I said. "This is. I like Jules," I said.

"Of course you do," she said. "Jules is wonderful. He's very nice to you."

"If it weren't for him, I would die of boredom."

I had already fallen in love with Jules, but did not tell Sophie. I couldn't trust her not to mock my emotions, though she certainly had some idea of how I felt. I talked of nothing but Jules, nothing but of my days with him. My interest in art had picked up. I could now talk about the light in Matisse's early work. I could tell you that he had not left France during the war because of a devoted sense of patriotism and sense that his life purpose lay in France. It was during the war that he moved from his Cimiez above Nice to Vence. I read the sports newspaper *L'Équipe* almost daily. I knew the role of the *peloton*. I moved the dial on Grandfather's radio to hear the broadcasts of the bicycle races and kept up with the results.

"Don't be so dramatic. Your life is your life," she paused. "Don't go about dying for someone else."

Mathilde screeched and Sophie turned to see what the problem was. I didn't care. Something was always setting her off.

Mathilde was afraid of every creature in nature, even ones that did not exist. She did a jerky dance every time she reached for a lemon. The wicker basket swung around her knees and she, thinking she was being stung or attacked, screamed, and ran back to the kitchen.

The cook sent her out again.

She approached the fruit trees with great trepidation as if they were a pack of lions ready to pounce on her.

"Go help Mathilde," Sophie said.

"She doesn't like my help," I said.

"She probably doesn't like your help, but she needs it," Sophie said. "Cook is fed up with her fears and nerves. She's been threatening to quit if we don't do something to change Mathilde."

"Then send Mathilde away," I said. "She's always moaning about being homesick. She misses Normandy. Cook says she talks about nothing but going back."

"I would be happy to send her home," Sophie said. "But she's afraid of the train. How can I get her up north if she won't get on a train?"

"Can't she walk?" I asked.

"To Paris?" she asked. "That would be really far, wouldn't it?"

"People walk there all the time," I said. "At least they used to."

"Really?" Sophie asked. "And when was that?"

"Back in the old days, before cars. They walked or rode their horses," I said.

"We don't own any horses so I guess she's here to stay," Sophie said. "Go. Go help her." She pushed her hip into mine, sending me out across the garden.

I did as Sophie told me to do, because that was the nature of our relationship. Seven years my senior, she had been telling me what to do since our mother died.

Mathilde looked up as I crossed the garden. She was suspicious of my offer to help as it wasn't my normal character.

"What do you want?" she asked.

Lest she think I was there of my own volition, I told her that Sophie had sent me.

She was reluctant to give up the basket, afraid possibly that I had come out to trick her. I reached up and began to pull the lemons from the branch. They were ripe—ready and easy to pick. I tossed them over to her and after two or three hit her legs, she handed me the basket.

"How many does the cook want?" I asked.

"Plenty," Mathilde answered.

"What is she making?"

"How would I know?" Mathilde asked. "I'm not in charge of the kitchen."

Mathilde danced about and I told her to keep still.

"Impossible," she said. "Not in the garden. It's never a good idea to keep still in a garden."

"The lemons can't hurt you," I said. "How can you be afraid of fruit?"

"It's not the fruit that has me worried," she said. "Bumblebees. Look, they're everywhere." She had never been stung; she spoke as if the threat was a forgone conclusion. "I will become very ill. I might die," she painted the scene with gestures. "I will blow up like a large mammal and then I will die."

Mathilde had the habit of humming when she was not talking. It was like a cat's purr, a constant undercurrent of noise.

Mathilde had been my mother's maid and it was for this reason that I made fun of her; I envied the relationship she had had with my mother. Mathilde had been very young when my mother hired her. She had extremely curly hair that she cut close to her head. Mother called her "my young lamb," and cooed at her as if Mathilde was a house pet. I resented their relationship, their closeness, the fact that Mathilde had a reason to go into my mother's room every day, that Mathilde was useful and that my mother appreciated the things she did for her.

When my mother died I was seven. She had been ill for such a long time that it was a shock to all of us when she went to the hospital one Sunday and died within the hour. Her illness had defined my world. Hushed hallways, whispered greetings, doctors' visits. When visiting friends or cousins, I was always surprised to see their mothers laughing and eating at the dinner table. My mother got out of bed so rarely that I never found it comforting or promising to see her standing.

The war had deeply saddened her. She talked with real despair about a life lost to such troubles and even after it ended, she couldn't force herself to admit that things might improve. The war took her desire to live; she gave up. The doctor said her weakness was not just physical and had she been determined to get well, she could have. "I think it's what she wanted," Father said when he told me and Sophie that Mother was dead. "We must accept that this is what she wanted."

I don't know if we did accept her death, but what choice did we have? She was gone.

Mathilde acted as if her own mother had died. She wailed at the funeral, confusing the priest who mistook her for my sister Sophie. He held her shoulders and consoled her until my father had to get up and tell the priest he was comforting my mother's maid, not her daughter. Consumed with grief, Mathilde hid herself away in the clothes cupboard, refusing to come out until my father said he would fire her if she didn't stop acting like a stray dog.

I disliked that she had been closer to my mother than I had. I sometimes thought I'd hire a beehive to hover outside her bedroom window. I'd lace her pillowcase with honey and see if they wouldn't swarm to her head. I had no idea where she got the idea that she would swell up like a large mammal, but for all I cared, she could swell up like a whole herd of elephants.

I picked lemons. Mathilde danced about.

When I finished, I handed her the basket. She told me Cook wanted it inside.

"Maybe you could take it in to her," I suggested.

"What if a bee follows me in?"

I ended up doing it myself.

Cook was cutting vegetables. She did not look up when I walked in, but began commenting without stopping: "She's amazingly good at getting others to do her work."

I laughed. I had to admire Mathilde. She did have a way of getting me to help with her chores.

I walked down the hall and saw that Sophie was in the study whispering with Grandfather. The door was open or I would have stood outside and listened. It was tiring living in a house where things were not discussed openly.

I went up to my room and waited for something awful to happen.

A half-hour later, Sophie danced in. She had changed out of her robe and was now wearing a clean pressed white skirt and a white blouse. She played with her aqua and orange silk scarf, which she tied around her waist.

"Where are you going?" I asked.

"You, too," she said.

"Really?" I asked. I was puzzled and turned to her for an explanation.

"Of course you're coming. I wouldn't leave you here alone."

"With Jules?"

"How many other men do we know who drive black Cadillacs?"

I got up and went to the window. Below was Jules' car. I had not heard him pull up, a noise that usually got my heart fluttering. Jules was rubbing the passenger side door down with a chamois. The door sparkled in the afternoon sunlight. He turned as if he could feel my eyes on him.

"Coming?" he asked.

"Of course," I called down, then turned back to Sophie and asked about Grandfather. "Will he be upset?"

"It's all set," she said. "You don't have to worry anymore about Jules. Grandfather's given us permission to go with him."

"You work miracles, Sophie," I said and jumped up.

"Get dressed," Sophie said. She went to the mirror and admired herself. She twirled and her skirt billowed out, upsetting the few things I had on my bureau.

I told her she looked beautiful.

"I do, don't I?" she asked. No one was a greater admirer of my sister than Sophie herself.

My sister had two wildly contrasting moods. The first was captivating, full of life and fun. She had enormous energy and drive and we were always up to something fun and exciting. The second was dark, pensive. In these moods, it was best to simply leave her alone. She was intolerable. Snappish, foul-tempered, you could not remind her that only twenty-four hours before she had been standing on a beach chair singing about the joys of a southern sun.

She was also several months pregnant, though with each passing day I became more confused about the truth of the supposition.

Things were a puzzle that year, and would have been much simpler if everyone had treated me like an adult. Considering the circumstances, I didn't understand why I wasn't given more of an opportunity to show that I could be as mature as any adult. Instead I was kept in the dark about most things.

Take, for instance, the scandal that brought us to the Côte d'Azur—the scandal was never fully explained to me. I used the word scandal because that was the word my father used when he told us we would be leaving Paris.

"I can't have you living here," he said. Father was furious, but I didn't know why. He had been yelling ever since I came home from school. I came into the apartment and heard him on the telephone.

I heard him talking to his close friend, Jean-Yves, a lawyer who he went to when he needed help. "What can I do?" I heard him ask. "What will people say? What will they think?"

A moment later. "Of course I can't help what people think. But it's not right." A very long pause. "It could happen again. Why not?"

I knocked on his door and announced that I was there. He sent me out for the evening meal's bread and when I returned with it, he looked surprised. "Who can think about food at a time like this?"

He assembled the three of us, Sophie, Grandfather, and me, in the main room and told us he had made a decision. "It is a final decision," he said. "I will not be talked out of it."

Grandfather was also angry, but less verbal about his rage. He sat with his hands on either side of his chair, mumbling about injustices.

"I will not have this scandal ruining our family," he said.

I knew no one who had suffered from scandals. My life was not exciting like that. But I read books where I learned that scandal meant sex and that it usually involved an unwanted baby.

I put the pieces together as best as I could. Sophie was guilty. She was young, attractive, and her desire for a love affair was one of her primary occupations.

I assumed Sophie was pregnant.

Father was moving us to the south of France. "For my own peace of mind."

"We're moving?" I asked. "All of us? Why? I don't understand. What happened?"

"No more questions. No more protests," Father said. "This is the way it will be."

"How can there be no more questions?" I asked. "We haven't had any in the first place."

It wasn't my scandal. Why was I being sent away? I didn't persist down those lines of questioning, as I wasn't sure that I didn't want to be sent away. Maybe it was a good thing. But with no information it was hard to know how to feel, how to react.

Grandfather wanted to know how long we'd be gone.

"I'm very tired," Father said.

"How long. Where? Why?" I asked. "What about my schooling? What's going to become of me? What about you? What will you do here all by yourself?" I could have continued, but Father cut me off.

"I think we've talked enough for one night."

"I agree," Sophie said. She got up with calm and a great deal of grace. Sophie was the kind of person who acted as if a camera was recording her every move. She was doing it that night. Before leaving, she stopped and bent down to kiss Grandfather's face. Her long dark hair spilled over him. "Don't worry. Things will work out for the best."

I didn't accept her cheerful philosophy. This was my future my father was changing and I demanded to know more. "South? South of where? South of what? Are we staying in France?"

I knew of the house near Menton. It was a family house, built by my father's relations. Our family had used it before the war, before my mother's illness, and was therefore a place Sophie remembered, but one I knew from stories. The Riviera was a vacation destination. People before did not go to the south in the wintertime. It just wasn't done.

Father was tight lipped. He held up his hands and pleaded fatigue.

I stayed up half the night trying to understand the situation. When my aunts and cousins talked of scandal, they gossiped and talked, speculating on one aspect of the situation, then another.

But our scandal was silent and secretive. Sex, in itself, did not seem to warrant the three of us being sent to the South of the country. Unwanted, unexpected babies were always scandals. So was murder, but I didn't know of anyone who had died. I stuck to the theory about the baby.

I decided that Sophie had made love to a man she could not marry, one my novels would have called inappropriate. Maybe he loved her, maybe she loved him but using the word scandal meant that there was something bad about him. An inappropriate man. This was it, I determined. This was the scandal. Had he been an appropriate man, we would have been planning a wedding, not planning a move south. I contemplated all the men I knew, trying to concentrate on the ones Sophie talked about. But while Sophie was always looking for love, she never spoke of having it. She was a strongheaded woman and talked about men with confidence and savvy. "I want my husband to be dark and very, very tall. I want people to stop what they're doing and take notice when we walk in a room."

Sophie and I went to the cinema all the time and one of her favorite things to do was to rewrite the endings of American films.

"Ilsa made a mistake," she told me.

"She did what she had to do. It was wartime," I said. "She made a decision. It was extremely noble."

"I would not have left Casablanca," she told me. "I would have told my skinny heroic husband that I was going to go with him but at the last moment, just before the plane takes off, I would have run off the plane and raced across the airstrip to Rick."

"That would have ruined the feel of the ending," I said. "The film was supposed to show the loss people suffered in the war. To show that their choices did not always guarantee them personal happiness."

"But my choice would give me what I want."

I didn't pull the baby idea from thin air. I had my reasons for thinking Sophie was pregnant. Our Paris apartment was not large. Sophie and I shared a room and one night she sneaked into the room and came over to my bed. She stood over me checking to make sure I was asleep. I pretended I was. She went over to the dressing table and took off her blouse. She had tape across her stomach. She yelped when she pulled it off.

"What is it?" I asked.

"Nothing. Go back to bed."

She had dimmed the light, but continued pulling the tape from her body. I guessed she was covering up her growing breasts, her enlarged stomach. I assumed she was hiding her changing body shape from Father.

I understood that Sophie had to be sent away, but it was confusing to me why I was going and especially confusing why Grandfather had to leave.

*T*he train trip was exciting, giving me hope that the south wouldn't be entirely miserable. I had images in my head of olive and lemon trees, of warm breezes, and of beaches. I concentrated on this instead of the oddness of the situation. We left the station at midnight, which I found to be exotic much like the narratives I read where everything happened after dark.

A porter helped us carry our bags onto the train. He flirted quickly and forcefully with Sophie who coyly pretended not to notice.

"Is that your nanny?" he asked me.

"My sister," I answered, but I was wasting my breath in correcting him.

"Aren't you lucky to have such a beautiful nanny?"

"I must be," I said.

"Does she have a name?"

"She does," I said. "And she has a voice too."

Sophie was happy and amused; her desire to be admired was constant. She skipped ahead so he could view her backside, a feature of which she was unnecessarily proud.

"Yes," the porter remarked. "I'd say she's very charming."

"Very beautiful, very charming and she quite resembles my father," I said. "See for yourself."

I pointed to Father, walking a few feet behind us. To the last minute Grandfather was reluctant to leave Paris and Father was practically pulling him along.

"I don't want to die down there," he told Father. "It's too far, almost a different country."

"Then don't," Father said.

"Don't?"

"Don't die," Father said.

"I'm afraid I have no control over that sort of thing. When I die, I die. And now I guess I'll die a lonely and broken man."

Father said there was no reason for such dramatic statements. "When you're ready to die, you can write me and I'll send you the money for a train ticket home."

"Please?" Grandfather asked. "What can I say that will make you change your mind?"

"Nothing." Their voices were loud and echoed in the vacuous space of the railway station. Father bought a ticket and came down the platform to see us off.

"Then I'm begging you to reconsider."

"I can't have you living here," Father said. "I have my career to think about."

I had considered that the father of the baby was a friend of Father's. Sophie often went out with Father and his bank clients and I wondered if she had gone against Father's wishes and slept with one of them. It didn't make exact sense. Father had often encouraged Sophie to date his friends. He wanted her to have a secure future. Maybe the man was married and his wife was barren. She had discovered a letter in her husband's suit coat, a letter from my sister wherein she revealed the great news of the upcoming infant. The wife, longing for a baby of her own, had demanded that my Father hand over Sophie's baby the minute it was born. Father, never before concerned with our family heritage, balked at the idea. There had to be dozens and dozens of married men with barren wives in Paris, almost all of Father's friends were married, some with children, some without, so I had no real suspects.

Sophie and I had set up our beds and I looked forward to a night of talk and discussions. I was sure that in our railway compartment, she would confide in me and I would learn the source of the scandal.

But then the soldiers boarded.

"Oh my," Sophie said. We stood and watched as they came down the corridors, hundreds of them pouring onto the train.

We determined, from snooping on their conversations, that they were on their way to Avignon. Sophie flirted. She smoked and drank with them. The night passed quickly and then suddenly we were on the platform in Nice waiting for the local train to take us into Menton.

Grandfather had spent the night in the gentlemen's car. He looked pale and shaky—smelled of cigarettes and brandy.

Sophie scolded him. She sounded so much like Father, I thought at first she might be mocking him.

"You don't look good," she said. "Did you get any sleep?"

"I don't like to sleep on trains," Grandfather said as if he was a frequent traveler. I knew this was his first time away from Paris in years.

"You're going to be very tired today."

"I met some very nice people. They were extremely sympathetic."

"I hope you haven't been up talking all night," she said to Grandfather.

"My business is my business."

"Not if you're talking about our business," she said. "There are some things that are meant to be private."

"And who decides that?"

I thought Grandfather dreadful. How could he tell strangers, especially strangers on a train, about Sophie's indiscretion? How awful that people who did not know our family name knew that my sister was in a family way?

*T*he house was dismal. The Villa Les Lianes was named for the thick vines that grew everywhere on the walled-in property. They twisted and turned and were impossible to control. They choked the lemon trees and killed many of them. The ochre-colored villa in the foothills was in need of repair. It was spacious but dirty. Dust blew down from the mountains every morning, so cleaning the table just to eat was a daily ritual. Older than our Paris apartment, it was much more isolated because of the groves—olive and fruit trees surrounding it.

Mathilde and Cook had been sent ahead. But when we got there we found that they had done nothing to prepare for our arrival. Cook said they had been overwhelmed.

"It's too much for me," Cook complained to Sophie. "I am stunned with the amount of work that this place entails."

"There's no hurry," Sophie said. "We have all the time in the world."

Predictably Mathilde had a hard time with the change. And the move threw her into a complete muddle. Either that, or as Cook claimed, she was extremely clever about getting out of doing work. Father might have fired her, but Sophie and I just rolled our eyes and complained about her nervous state.

To Cook, Mathilde was just another one of the trials she had to live with in this new situation.

"From the moment we got on the train, that girl has been nothing but trouble," Cook said, then gave us every detail of their trip south, which consisted of Mathilde crying, Cook ignoring her show of emotions.

In Paris, Cook had been employed by three families in our building. She was a gossipy woman and liked to talk to one family about the other. I didn't care to know that the woman who lived below us only changed the bedsheets once a month, but Cook was thrilled to tell me. I don't know what she thought about our family but when Father offered her the chance to travel to the south with us and help set up the house, she readily accepted. It was temporary; her plan was to spend six or seven months with us and then return to Paris.

I understood Cook's sense of bewilderment at trying to clean such a large dirty house and grounds. I had never been to a house that had been shut up for so many years. It sounded simple—pull back the shutters, open the windows, and let in the light, but the work was tremendous, especially as we were opening the house in the middle of winter. The days were short. They were over before we even got started.

Les Lianes was filthy, the upstairs overrun with mice and

hedgehogs who had nested there. Large gray pigeons that ate the neighbor's gardens flew in and out of the windows as if they owned the place.

The furniture was still covered and smelled of old people and mothballs. It was not what I had imagined and I resented it for being different than my image of a villa in the south of France should have been.

December on the Riviera was rainy and cold. January was worse. I wrote to friends back home, but found it hard to write more than a few lines. What could I tell them? I realized that we were friends because we shared the same experiences. And without school, I had nothing to share with them.

The rain clouds came and hung over the mountaintops. The air was gray. The Villa was dark and damp. I was bored. Mathilde had a cold. Cook had the flu. Grandfather was miserable. Only Sophie seemed cheerful. She cleaned and moved things. She got rid of the hedgehogs. She had a real sense that a bit of work would make everything right.

I tried to ask Sophie about the baby, but her answers were vague. She didn't avoid my questions, but she didn't enlighten me either. Months had passed since my world had been changed so dramatically, but I knew nothing more than I had when Father first told us we were leaving Paris.

I knew what pregnant women looked like, they grew large and awkward and cranky. They put their hands in the middle of their backs and complained of pain and heartburn. They took to their beds, they moaned. They obsessed with their health and feared for the health of their baby. They did not walk around with a bucket of soapy water like a street cleaner, sighing and talking about how beautiful the patio would be in the summer months.

Then spring came. The change of season was so quick, so unlike the slow wet springs I knew from Paris, that I didn't trust it to last. But it did. The Mediterranean was suddenly alive with color. The heat warmed everything. Our Villa, I realized, had been painted so that it could catch the sunlight and in the afternoon the outside walls shone like glass. It was a magical time of day, something I hadn't realized in the winter months. Radio Riviera, the local station, played dance music all day long. I memorized the jingles of the advertisements. Sophie and I danced about, our bare feet on the rocks and gravel of the drive.

The scent of citrus hung in the air, growing more pungent as the days grew warmer.

And then, of course, we met Jules.

Chapter Two

*W*e met Jules one day in Monte Carlo. We had spent the morning combing the shore for lost treasure. The raging storms of the past weeks had convinced Sophie that there were ships in trouble out on the sea and she determined that we could find something of value if only we looked.

"What are we looking for?" I asked.

"Pirates," Sophie answered. "Pirate ships."

"There haven't been pirate ships for centuries," I said. I was certain that everything in the world had already been discovered. There were no more ships. No more walking the plank, treasure maps, "shiver me timbers." All that was gone, existing now only in the imaginations of little kids.

Sophie disagreed. "You never know what'll go over when disaster strikes."

I thought she might be hoping for a man overboard, but didn't see the appeal of finding bodies washed up along the coastline.

But it didn't really matter to me what we were doing. It was enough just to be on the beach. I thought we were spending too much time cleaning up the Villa.

Sophie had decided that she wanted Les Lianes to look like it had before the war. "As it did in my youth," she ruminated. She was beginning to sound like Grandfather. "This was not the way it was," he chanted like a song refrain. According to Grandfather, the entire

Riviera had changed and not for the better. Nothing was as good as it had been when he was younger.

"Which is why we must work," Sophie said. "We must make it like it was before."

"We'd need an army," Grandfather said.

Cook agreed with him. "To fix this place up would be an impossible feat."

"Don't say that," Sophie scolded. "It will take some work, but I see it as it was years ago when Mother was alive. It was beautiful."

"I don't see anything beautiful about this place now," Cook said. "There were squatters here during the war. They ruined everything."

Sophie, the optimist, made schedules for all of us.

"Italians," Cook continued. "If you want my guess. I'd say the people who stayed here all these years were Italians."

We didn't really know if there had been squatters. People had been in, and they had taken things, but we were surprisingly lucky. We heard tales from the neighboring houses about being robbed clean to the baseboards. Men came in and took sinks, faucets, light fixtures, window frames.

My sister was very organized, but after a few weeks it was obvious that we could surface clean the place, but that for everything else, we would need help. The problem with Les Lianes was that it was old; it needed repairs as much as cleaning. I helped Sophie collect the names of contractors in the area and we made appointments to have them give us estimates on the work that needed to be done. While this was being done, we found our days free. We usually went down the mountain and explored the seashore. I didn't care what we did—sit in the sun, sit in a café, ride the buses, window shop—but it did get a bit boring with just Sophie and me.

The coastline was rocky and Sophie walked on the water's edge, her shoes tied around her neck, her hat held on with one hand. The Mediterranean, not ruled by tides, was turbulent that afternoon. The sky was a brilliant blue and there were a number of people getting sun that afternoon. Sophie bent over and caught hold of a floating object in one grand swoop of her arm. She lifted it over her head.

"Agnes, Agnes," she called. "Look."

I waved, but did not get up. I was half sitting on my chair, half sitting on the beach. Underneath the top layer of pebbles and rocks was a thick coating of black grime—the dust off the mountains. Regardless of the dirt, I thought it might be fun to bury my feet in the beach.

"Come quick," she commanded.

It was not like Sophie to fish with her bare hands.

Sophie shouted and waved her discovery at me, immediately attracting notice of the other sunbathers. She loved being the center of attention; she was probably very happy. I strained to see what she was holding. It looked like a wine bottle, but hoped she didn't plan on drinking it.

The rocks and gravel shifted beneath Sophie's feet and she scurried up the beach like a crab losing ground.

The boy who worked the beach rushed over. Normally, he was a lazy sort. He stood near his stack of lounge cushions and got up only if you asked three or four times for a cushion; then he'd follow you down acting as if it was the most tiresome chore. But somehow Sophie finding the empty wine bottle had inspired him. He was full of energy and curiosity.

"What is it?" the beachboy asked. "What did you find?"

"Look," Sophie said and presented the wine bottle as if it was some kind of exotic treasure.

"Is it empty?" I asked, but Sophie only smiled at her discovery.

Others wandered over, some came closer than others.

A small man wearing a pressed linen shirt came up and offered his assistance. This was Jules and I had noticed him before. He was sitting a few chairs down from Sophie and me. He had an oversized sketchbook balanced on his knees and from the moment we had sat down, he kept looking over at us. Thinking that he was sketching us, I let my head scarf go and ran behind the chairs to fetch it. I looked at his page. There were a few black lines that perhaps were meant to be the ocean, but the rest of the page was completely blank. He was not drawing Sophie or me but staring at us, because he was curious. I told him we were fine. We didn't need anyone's help or assistance. I didn't waste energy being polite.

"There's something inside," the beachboy said. "Look. There is something in the bottle."

Sophie was out of breath from her short walk up the beach. She held up her hand as if asking the men to allow her to catch her breath then started talking a mile a minute as if she had all the air in the world.

"I think it's money," she said and slid a stick down the slim neck to help her ease the paper out. "This close to the casinos, you never know what will happen."

Even my sister could not convince me that someone would throw money into the sea.

The note was written in pencil:

> "*Help. I'm being held captive.*
> *This is not a joke.*
> *I'm in great danger and fear*
> *for my life. Do not wait to take*
> *action. It may already be too late.*
> *The name of the boat is . . .*"

The end of the last sentence had either been erased in the salt water or had never been written.

"What should we do?" Sophie asked.

"About what?" I asked.

"About the note," Sophie said.

The winds had calmed and the sun was extremely warm. The circle of sunbathers had changed into a circle of advice, everyone inching closer to Sophie who read the note for a second time.

"Why do we have to do anything?" I asked. "Toss it back in the water. We'll go home. Or go eat lunch. That's what I'd like to do."

"Did you read the note?" Sophie asked. "It's a call for help. Someone's life is in danger."

"You don't really believe that, do you?" I wasn't sure what she was up to, but she was up to something.

"Imagine the danger he might be in," Sophie said.

"Who?" I asked.

"Him," she said and pointed to the note.

"Who are we talking about?"

"The person in trouble, Agnes," Sophie said. "You can't ignore someone's call for help. This is serious. We must help him."

Much to my surprise, the group did not dismiss the bottle and the note as I wanted them to. They clucked their opinions and advice, all of them talking at once. Sophie stood in the center, basking in the attention. She wore a light pink skirt with a matching blouse, which she had tied in a knot at her waist. It was a calculated look, not something you'd normally think to wear sunbathing.

I was the only one who found anything amusing about the note.

"A bored sailor," I told the group. "Drank a bottle of wine, felt like playing a joke, and wrote the note. He probably passed out just as he tossed the bottle overboard."

I stood up and took a few steps forward, trying to imitate a drunk. No one laughed. They turned their attention back to Sophie.

The beach boy jumped on his bike and rode to the crest of the hill for a better look at the ocean—their view from the beach was limited to the bay.

He came back and breathlessly explained that there was a large ship on the horizon. It was moving east, towards Italy.

People reported that they thought the ship on the horizon was the same one that had docked in Villefranche-sur-Mer last night.

The crowd insisted that the police be notified. If not, the boat might cruise into international waters where it would be confused with other ships. Someone ran off again, this time to the town's police station, a room in the city hall building.

We went to the Café de Paris, a fancy place on the boardwalk.

Our group from the beach quickly filled the tables. Drinks were ordered and offered and suddenly it was an impromptu celebration of sorts.

The police came. They assured Sophie and the worried group of sunbathers that they would do everything they could.

"Which means what?" I asked. "What can they do? Check every boat in the ocean to see if anyone drank a bottle of wine last night?"

Sophie was in her glory. She shook hands with the police and expressed her appreciation for their prompt and thorough attention.

With the police came a man from the local news, who wanted to get a photograph of the big discovery. Sophie stuck the note back inside the bottle and posed.

"Grandfather will see the paper," I warned her. "Maybe he'll show it to Father."

It seemed like all this would get us into trouble.

"Don't be silly," Sophie said. "Grandfather doesn't care about the rest of the world. If it's not his business, it's not his concern."

"This wouldn't make him happy," I said.

"Then we won't tell him, will we?" she asked. "There's no reason to make him even more miserable than he is."

An Irish Wolfhound wandered into the press photograph, his hair wet and dirty. Sophie, on the other hand, looked stunning.

*T*he press left, the police left, everyone else went home, everyone promising to keep their ears open for news of any trouble on one of the big ships. Sophie and I were left with the empty wine bottle and the note.

She sat back in her chair, entirely pleased with herself. "That was fun," she sighed. She sipped from her champagne, then encouraged me to drink my glass.

"It will put great color in your checks," she told me. "There's nothing wrong with a woman who drinks. It shows she's healthy."

She drank from her glass. "Healthy and daring. I like men to think of me as daring."

"Aren't you?" I asked.

"Not as much as I'd like them to think of me." My sister swatted at her legs. "Bees," she said. "Mathilde would be miserable here."

"I can't see Mathilde on the beach," I said.

"She'd hate it," Sophie agreed.

"It's too warm," I said. "She'd melt." I had an image of Mathilde in her black uniform, her sensible dark shoes, her worried expression made even more severe by the frivolity of the sunbathers.

"It went better than I thought it would," Sophie said.

I had the note from the bottle in my hand. I read it again trying to see if I found anything urgent or real about the message. A third read and I recognized the penmanship. Sophie had a very distinct way of capitalizing certain letters.

"You wrote this yourself," I said and shoved the note across the café table.

She laughed but picked it up and pocketed it. "Don't be silly."

I wasn't wrong. "You did. You wrote that note."

She nodded and then as if we were co-conspirators, talked over what she had done. "It was clever, wasn't it? No one else suspected it was a fake. Even the police. I thought they'd sense it wasn't a real note."

"Why?" I asked.

"Because it's what they do," Sophie said. "They root out criminals. They look for false truths. It's their job."

"I meant why did you write the note?" I asked.

"That's what we call a white lie," she said and shrugged her shoulders. She was already quite bronzed and had pulled her shirt off her shoulders. "I call it harmless," Sophie said. "Fun. A sporting game on such a lovely afternoon."

I fiddled with the ashtray, then carelessly let the whole thing—cigarette butts, ashes—spill. It quickly dirtied the entire tabletop. Black grime, just like the beach.

Sophie was my sister and I loved her, but I felt her reckless behavior was partially at my expense. If she had planned the prank, why didn't she tell me about it beforehand? Why did I have to discover it for myself? I didn't like feeling left out.

"You're not at all like me," Sophie said. The ashes on the table-top scattered over to her side. A moment later, she stuck her elbow in it and a long black smudge appeared. I checked my skin and found it just as dirty. I wiped it across the dark print of my skirt.

"Maybe I'm not," I told her. "And maybe that's a good thing."

I hadn't meant to ruin the afternoon by bickering with her. She could get into such a pout if you didn't agree with her. I sighed and told her I was sorry.

"Next time, tell me before you plan something like this," I said.

"That's fair," she agreed and flashed me a smile.

"Friends?" I asked.

She pulled on my pinkie finger.

She lit another cigarette just as the man at the next table began clapping his hands. We turned to see what had caught his attention only to discover that it was us.

"Brava. Brava," the skinny little man at the next table wasn't just clapping, he was applauding. "A wonderful show. Simply splendid."

He came over and asked if he could join us.

No one said he could, but he did anyway.

He was beaming. "Madame, you're a genius," he addressed Sophie. "I must tell you that at first I had my doubts. I thought there was something odd about your seaside discovery."

I recognized him. He was the man from the beach. The one with the enormous sketch pad and no talent.

"But then I thought no," the man continued. He was animated, words tumbling out of his mouth. "Only a professional actress could keep the charade up as long as you did."

Sophie was coy. "I don't know what you're talking about."

"Of course you do," he insisted.

"I think you're mistaken."

But he had heard our conversation. There seemed little point in trying to deny it. Finally she accepted the compliment with a slight bow of her head. "Thank you very much," she said. "Many many thanks. I'm glad someone can appreciate my work."

They acted as if they were discussing a theatrical performance.

I swatted the bees from the lip of my champagne glass. Then saw that they weren't bees, but wasps. Large, dark menacing wasps, who probably had a nest nearby.

"Allow me to introduce myself. My name is Jules Agard. I am a resident of the Riviera."

I remembered his introduction because at the time I was struck by the quirky way he explained who he was. "We're newcomers," Sophie explained. "Living in a gloomy old family house up in the hills above Menton."

"Ah, Menton," Jules said. "A sleepy little town."

"Sleepy?" Sophie snorted. "It's dull as mud."

"That's what they say," Jules asked.

"Ghastly," she said. "Worse than you can imagine."

She waved away a huge wasp sucking the rim of her glass, then told him our names.

"Are you from Paris?"

"Do we look like we're from Paris?" Sophie said. She wore her blue top, the one that matched her eyes. She had twisted her hair on top of her hand and fastened it with a clip that had belonged to our mother. The matching bracelet was pushed above her elbow, an odd, but exotic place to wear jewelry.

"We're from Paris," I told him. Why play games with a man who had difficulties sketching the ocean?

"I knew it," Jules said. "Let me be the first to welcome you to the south of France."

"We've been here for weeks," I said. "If you wanted to welcome us, you should have done it earlier."

"My baby sister," Sophie introduced me, but he was not interested in me.

Jules raised my champagne glass and toasted Sophie's brilliant—it had now been elevated to brilliant—performance. "Bravo," he said and drained my glass.

Sophie raised her glass. I saw the wasp on the rim, but didn't warn her.

She put the glass to her lips to sip.

Everything went wild when the wasp stung her bottom lip.

The table went over, the glasses, the water carafe, the wine bottle, which I had thought to be empty, but I could see the spill of champagne circling the broken glass.

Sophie cried out in real pain.

The waiter ran to Sophie's side and I thought he meant to help her up. Instead he stood over her and yelled.

"You have caused enough commotion for one day," he said.

It was my fault; I should have warned her about the wasp on her glass. She might be a liar and a silly woman, but there was no reason for me to be petty and mean-spirited.

"You must pay," the waiter said. He knelt down and wagged his finger at her face. "You must pay for all this."

"She was attacked," I said. "Vicious wasps attacked her."

The waiter was adamant. "She must pay for the damage."

She still had her hand to her lip and I thought she might be bleeding. I hoped she was, as this would show the waiter that he was being rude.

Jules Agard had disappeared, which infuriated me. One minute he was trying to charm Sophie, the next he was gone. He who thought her daring performance so commanding had fled the minute there was trouble.

I helped Sophie up.

She leaned on me and we walked in the opposite direction of the café. "Stop," the waiter called. "I will call the police."

A moment later, she swooned.

"Oh dear," she sighed as she pitched forward, then swayed back on her heels. Then she tipped all the way to one side: I had to really hold on or she would have fallen. Then like a springboard, she came back up and swayed to the opposite side. Her eyes were closed and her body went limp. I thought I could hold her, then realized I was not strong enough.

Then suddenly Jules was at my side. "Allow me," he said and scooped up Sophie in his arms and carried her across the street.

The waiter stopped at the end of the boardwalk and watched

Jules and Sophie disappear around the corner. Not wanting to be caught with the bill, I followed after them.

Jules was not a big man and he was obviously struggling as he walked Sophie away from the café.

"There's my car," he said.

"A car," Sophie said. "How convenient."

Jules gave a huge sigh as he reached the black Cadillac. Sophie tumbled out of his arms and into the front seat.

"Did you steal this?" I asked. It was a beautiful machine. I didn't know people who owned cars.

"Of course not," he said.

I looked around suspiciously. Jules did not seem the kind of man to own a car.

He nodded. "I promise you. It's mine." He offered to show me his papers.

"I don't think that will be necessary," I said.

Jules helped me climb over Sophie and into the back seat.

Then we were off, winding our way through the streets of Monte Carlo. Jules turned one way, but it dead-ended at a seawall.

Sophie, who had been resting her head against the back of the seat, opened her eyes when Jules stopped the car and began maneuvering the turnaround.

"Are we safe?" she asked.

"Have you been faking it?" I asked. "Was all that a performance?"

"Not entirely," she said. "I did get stung. But the fainting was my own creation."

"It got rid of that annoying waiter," Jules said.

"We've never been good friends," Sophie said.

"I see the artistic differences of your personality."

We turned away from the sea and ended into the hills above Menton. Jules stopped the car and we got out to admire the view.

Sophie's lip grew fatter. "I feel like I've just come back from the dentist," she said, her mouth all soft as if it was filled with cotton. Jules asked her if she was going to faint again. "I'm done fainting for the day," she said.

She claimed it was getting harder to talk, but she didn't stop.

"Not a word to Mathilde," Sophie warned me.

"Of course not," I said.

"And we'll keep Grandfather in the dark too," she said. "Maybe about all the day's events."

Just then Jules accelerated and my words were eaten up in the winds. I could have shouted anything and it wouldn't have mattered. Sophie had cupped her hair at the base of her neck so that it did not blow wild like mine. But I loved the sensation of the wind whipping my hair about.

Once we slowed to take the steep curves winding up towards Les Lianes, Jules told us about swarming—how the bees were upset and would not have attacked Sophie unless they thought their home was in danger. He thought it best if Sophie got a doctor to examine her.

"You're like a medicine book," Sophie teased. "Where do you store all your information?"

"Some things I know. Some things I make up," Jules said.

"A man after my own heart," Sophie said.

"I'm an amateur compared to you," Jules said.

I sat back and enjoyed the drive. We moved slowly away from the Mediterranean Sea. I was disappointed when the car slowed as he made the turn into gravel road leading towards the Villa.

Sophie thanked Jules and offered him money for the ride home.

"I'm insulted that you would even think of such a thing."

"Then you're a dear," Sophie said. "My knight in shining armor."

"Rescuing damsels in distress is one of the things I do best," Jules said. He got out and opened her door for her. Since we had no money, it was a good thing he didn't accept Sophie's offer to pay for our ride home.

We watched her as she walked up the steps and into the house. At the doorway, she turned and threw her arm across her forehead, a dramatic last gesture. Jules laughed.

Jules and I stood on the driveway. I picked up a fistful of gravel and let it sift through my fingertips.

Grandfather put his head out the study window. "Agnes," he said, his voice accusing me of doing something wrong simply by saying my name. "What are you doing?"

I picked up another handful of gravel and tossed it towards the house. "Experimenting with gravity," I said.

"Only a fool would play in the rain," he said. Jules found Grandfather's comment amusing. I didn't, for I knew he really did think me a fool.

The sky was filled with rain clouds, but it had not yet started to rain. Jules said it was time for him to be home. The thunderclouds hung overhead and the air was filled with electricity.

Grandfather had more to say. "Who's that standing beside you?"

"Jules," I called out.

"Jules?" Grandfather repeated.

"That's his name," I said. "Jules Agard."

"What's he doing here?"

"He's talking to me."

"I can see that," Grandfather said.

"Then why did you ask?" I said under my breath for Jules to hear.

"Where's Sophie?" Grandfather asked.

"Upstairs," I answered.

"Why?"

"She doesn't feel well."

"What's wrong with her?"

"Maybe we could continue this conversation later?" I asked.

Grandfather's head disappeared into the house.

I tossed my gravel around the tires of Jules' Cadillac. Jules took my hands and emptied them of pebbles much like a parent scolding a child. I blushed, apologizing. "Don't mind him," I said.

"Is that Sophie's husband?" Jules asked.

"Of course not," I laughed and Jules did too. "That's Grandfather. Grouchy old Grandfather."

Jules smiled. "And where is her husband?"

"She doesn't have one of those," I said. "That's one of the problems." I wasn't going to tell him about the scandal, not then. I wanted him to come back the next day. Driving in an open air car with the winds in our face was wonderful and I wanted to do it again. I thought he would stay away if he suspected anything strange in our lives.

"You could come back tomorrow," I suggested. "How would that be?"

"I'd love to," he said.

"You would?"

"I would," Jules said. "Give my best to your sister. I hope she's not too ill."

"She never is," I said.

"Wasp bites can be extremely dangerous," Jules told me.

"That's what you said."

"Did I?" Jules said. He put his fingers through his hair and brushed the short pieces from his forehead. "Repeating myself means I've gotten boring. Best to take my leave before I put you to sleep."

I asked him again if he planned to return.

"Now who's repeating themselves?" he asked.

Before getting in the car Jules shook my hand. Men didn't shake my hands and I was puzzled by his gesture of farewell.

The rain started before Jules had even left the property. Thick bloated raindrops fell. I listened to the engine as Jules meandered down the hillside. The horn wailed once or twice, then the afternoon fell silent. I was immediately bored.

The garden smelled of mimosa and jasmine. I felt strange, then realized that I was happy—something I hadn't felt in a long while.

*T*hat night, I came up with a plan.

It was a very simple plan and if it worked the way I envisioned, everyone would get what they wanted.

My plan was that Sophie fall in love with Jules; he was obviously intrigued by her.

They could fall in love. They could marry.

Jules could move into Les Lianes. Father would come down for the wedding. He could drive Mathilde back home with him. And

Grandfather could leave too. As there would be no more scandal, there would be no more reason for Grandfather to stay in a place he loathed.

After the baby came, I would drive around in the back of Jules' motor car with the picnic basket, minding that the bottles of wine and water didn't smash into each other. We would drive slowly trying to find an isolated, but beautiful place to lunch.

Chapter Three

*L*uckily, my foolish plan to have Jules and Sophie marry was not successful. They fawned over each other, but they were not in love.

People in love were shy with each other. They cuddled, they whispered, they demanded privacy. They did not parade their affections and passions as if it were a competition to see who could shout the loudest. They did not act like Sophie and Jules.

"I love you, darling," Sophie cooed.

"I love you back, darling," Jules answered.

Sophie and Jules had overheard a British couple on the beach, a middle-aged married couple, referring to each other as *Darling*. And from then on, they only called each other darling. It was annoying. *Darling* this, *darling* that.

To say that I was enthralled with Jules would have been an understatement. Like the Mediterranean itself, he was charismatic, charming, and utterly unique. Not knowing what else to do, I blamed Sophie for my tumultuous feelings.

"Don't act like that," I warned her.

"Like what?" she asked.

"So ditzy," I said. "Be interesting. Be daring and pretty, but most of all be interesting."

That's what I was trying to do.

"What are you worrying about?" Sophie asked. We were in Cannes where Jules had invited us on a boat ride. But I couldn't relax. Why didn't Sophie see that in a minute Jules could simply sour on us and then we'd be back up in the Villa cleaning the stained and always dusty tiles of the large foyer?

"Trust me," Sophie said. "We're going to have a great time this summer."

Sophie never had doubts. It was her steadfast refusal to let life dictate to her that I wanted to emulate, but could not.

"It's been a difficult year," Sophie said. "We deserve some fun. Things are going to work out. You'll see. I've been thinking quite a bit lately."

"About what?" I asked.

"All in good time," she promised and taking my arm, she steered me back to the beach where Jules was persuading the boat rental man that we needed a discount on the afternoon boat rental.

I was the worrier, the one who thought that if things were good, it wouldn't last. I considered that something bad was always waiting for us on the horizon.

*T*hat afternoon on the boat, Sophie demanded our attention. "I have something important to tell you," she said. "Listen."

"We're always listening to you, darling," Jules said.

"From now on," Sophie said, "we are no longer going to be wasting our time."

"Are you not happy with the boat ride?" Jules asked. "I thought you were enjoying yourself."

"The boat is incredible and you're divine," she said. "but I'm talking about our dreams."

"Who said we had dreams?" I asked.

Sophie was not to be led off track. "We're not going to waste our days on the beach, staring up at the sun, looking across the Mediterranean."

"We're not?" I asked.

"Why not?" Jules asked.

"It's bad enough that Agnes didn't go to school this year,"

Sophie said. " I can't have her doing nothing but beachcombing the next few months."

"I tried," I said. I had spent a few weeks in the local school. It was in Nice in the old section of town. The classroom was filled with the sons and daughters of the Russians who had come to the Riviera for medicinal purposes. The teacher, overwhelmed by the number of enrolled students, sat at his desk and played cards. When someone spoke or raised their hands, he demanded that they return to the lessons, though he didn't specify where we would find these lessons.

The teacher spoke several languages and often talked to us in Italian or Romanian. For no apparent reason, he would just begin a tirade in some foreign tongue. When asked what he was saying, he sneered and told us he was telling his war adventures. "Don't you want to teach us or test us on our knowledge?" a bold girl about my age spoke up. The teacher had flicked the cards and said no. "I'm sure you don't know a thing about the world." He went back to his card game and some of the older boys went to the window and jumped out. They ran down the street, the sounds of their footfalls growing fainter as they headed into the main market. A few minutes later, I left too. Not by the window—I used the door. I heard the teacher saying goodbye in Italian.

In Paris, school had been rigorous and challenging; the teachers knew everything about everything. It had been intimidating, but it had not felt like a waste. Like the cold winds and icy sidewalk, school did not belong on the Riviera.

"*I*'ve got our days organized," Sophie said. "From now on, they're going to have a purpose."

"This sounds tedious," Jules said. He gave me one of the oars and directed me to pull to the right. We were moving in circles and Jules said the rocking motion was beginning to upset his stomach. Another rental boat came too close to us and we hit. The gentleman mumbled his apology.

"Listen, darling," Sophie said. "You'll like what I have to say."

"I always do," Jules said. He paused as he considered this. "At least I always did."

"August," Sophie decided. "That's when we'll reach our goals. Before then is acceptable, but not later than."

"This sounds like work," Jules said.

"Of course it's work," Sophie said. "Obtaining one's goals is definitely a struggle. It has to be or else it's not worth it."

"What kind of goals are we going to go after?" I asked. When I thought about goals, I thought schoolwork. I was more interested in preparing a wedding party. Jules' face was puckered in displeasure.

"It depends on what you want," Sophie said. "Here, I'll start. My goal is to find a husband. By August, I want to know the man I'll marry."

Jules laughed. "That's fast work."

"I am very determined," Sophie said.

"Best of luck," Jules said and I gave her my good wishes too.

"Now it's your turn," she said.

"I want you to find a man too," I said. "I fully support your quest."

Jules laughed, then let go of the oar and I had to row over to catch it before the waves took it away.

"You have to find your own," Sophie said.

"My own man?" I asked. "I'm much too young to marry."

"Your own goal," Sophie said, then decided it would be best if we said our goals aloud. "For everyone to hear."

Jules and I had stopped rowing. We drifted about in the bay. Other boats passed; no one seemed to be working hard and the idea of setting goals seemed arduous.

"Come on, now," Sophie urged. "State them clearly and definitively so there's no vagueness or confusion about what you want."

"I don't need to have a goal." I said. "I'm only fifteen. I just want my life to be fun."

"I agree," Jules said. "I think Agnes has the right idea."

"She doesn't," Sophie said.

"That's an excellent goal," Jules said. "I couldn't agree with you more. Let's devote our lives to amusing ourselves."

"I hardly think that's worthwhile."

"But it is," I said. "What could be better than fun? There isn't a thing in the world more exciting."

"What do you really want, Jules?" Sophie asked. "What's your ambition?"

"I don't have any ambition."

"That's not right," Sophie clucked her tongue, but his carefree attitude was what I liked best about Jules.

*J*ules, unlike any adult male I had known, did not have a regular job.

"Don't you work?" I had asked him after knowing him only a few days. Jules was open and I didn't feel queer asking him such direct questions.

"Sometimes," he said. "Sometimes I do."

"But not every day?" I asked.

"No, no. Not even every week." This admission did not seem to embarrass him. He wasn't the least bothered by it.

"Why not?" I did not know men who didn't work. Not by choice. Grandfather had stopped working and he was miserable. Jules was the opposite of that, but he was young and in good health. I wondered if Jules had hurt himself in the war, then figured he was too young to have been in the war.

"That wouldn't suit me," Jules said.

"What do you do with your days?"

"I hang about," he said. "I look at things. I entertain myself. I allow myself to be entertained."

"That's it?"

"It certainly fills a day," he said. "And I'm hardly alone in my endeavors. Plenty of people in paradise do exactly what I do." That was what he called the Côte d'Azur. He blamed the weather and the sea. "It's too beautiful here."

"How do you live if you don't work?" I was practical and needed concrete responses to my questions.

"People like me aren't supposed to work." He pointed to his chest as if introducing me to a new species.

"And what kind of person are you?"

"An extremely happy one," Jules said.

My goal formed quickly and easily. I informed Sophie that I had decided how I was going to devote my time that summer.

"Brava. Brava," Sophie said. "I knew you could do it."

Jules called me a traitor. "I thought you were going to be lazy like me. I don't know if I can support the two of you working so hard."

I told him not to worry. "Mine shouldn't be hard work," I said. "At least I don't think it will be hard. It won't be work. That's for certain."

"Tell us what your goal is," Sophie said. "Let us hear the details and we'll decide if we approve of it for you." Sophie sat with her legs crossed. She worried that her legs looked fat when she crossed them and had decided that she would only cross them at her ankles.

"It's private," I said and then because I knew Sophie wouldn't be satisfied with this, explained that it was complicated. "But what's important is that I know what it is."

"But that's not fair."

"You never said we had to tell the whole world. Aren't they personal goals?"

"I guess that's all right." Sophie deemed her favor upon me.

"Of course it is," Jules said. "There's nothing wrong with Agnes having secrets. She's entitled."

I gave him a wide smile.

My goal was simple. I wanted Jules to find me attractive. I wanted him to throw his arms around me and shout, *I love you darling.* I wanted him to think me clever, to find me intriguing, to think me wildly exciting. I wanted Jules to appreciate me with the same strength that I appreciated him. I wanted Jules to desire me, to treat me romantically. I wanted to be the center of his universe, because he had become the center of mine. I wanted him to love me because I loved him.

"Agnes has her goal so it's your turn," Sophie demanded of Jules. "Maybe something to do with your art?"

"That would be futile," Jules said. "I'm not that talented."

"Then why do you drag that sketchbook everywhere we go?" Sophie asked.

"People are attracted to artists," Jules said. "And I am attracted to people."

"Maybe I should get a sketchbook," Sophie considered.

"I can loan you mine," Jules said.

"You won't ever be rich and famous?" I asked. I thought he might be.

"No one will ever know my name," Jules said. "Unless, of course, something goes terribly wrong in my life and I commit a crime. But I won't ever paint my way into fame."

I did not yet know about his obsession with Matisse. He hadn't yet confided in me. I didn't know people who dabbled in things. My life had been surrounded by hardworking people and the frivolity of doing something but not striving to be the best at it was a new idea for me. I found it decadent and thrilling that Jules would draw because it amused him. I knew that Jules was exactly the kind of person Grandfather would find intolerable and worthless and I grew even more enthusiastic in my goal.

*M*y first step in getting what I wanted that summer was to sabotage my sister. This was my first priority. She and Jules were not in love, but they did fawn over each other. Before Jules could notice me, I thought it best to end his fascination with Sophie.

I moved quickly.

It was Sophie's turn to take Grandfather to the doctor's. We shared the chore of those weekly trips. Grandfather's eyes were bad and they seemed to grow worse every day. He could not read the numbers on the buses or trams, he could not see the numbers on the buildings. That day was Sophie's turn. Jules picked me up and we went out.

Without Sophie, I was free to say what I wanted.

I attacked without warning.

"Do you know Sophie is with child?" I asked. I had heard pregnancy explained that way in a film and I thought it sounded ladylike, delicate. We were walking through the flower market in Nice. Jules had stopped to inquire on the price of the forsythias. The buckets were so packed with flowers in great blooms, it was hard to see the prices.

He didn't hear so I repeated myself. I was much louder and firmer. "Did you know?" I asked. "That my sister Sophie is with child?"

Jules threw back his head and laughed. "That's marvelous," he said.

I was not pleased by his reaction and wondered if he had misunderstood. Maybe I wasn't using the expression in the right way. "That's a strange reaction to a very serious problem," I said.

The woman selling forsythias picked up a bunch and began to wrap them in newspaper. Jules and I moved away. Flowers were an extravagance our pocketbooks didn't allow. Besides, as Jules had said, what was the point of taking the flowers away when they looked so beautiful and so plentiful packed into the buckets and lined up in the numerous stalls?

I wanted to shock him. If he wasn't going to marry Sohpie, than there was no reason for him to think her beautiful and clever. He could think me beautiful and clever.

Jules laughed. "With child?" He danced ahead, stopping to smell the mimosas, which did look weaker once cut from their branches.

"I don't think it's anything to laugh at," I said. "It's a very serious condition. My Father wasn't laughing when he discovered her secret."

"Unless I'm totally mistaken, I think you misunderstood what someone said," Jules said.

"How would I have misunderstood something like that?" I asked.

I wanted him to dismiss Sophie, to call her foolish. I wouldn't have cared if he was shocked by her indecent behavior. Anything but his insistence that I was wrong.

"You don't know my family or our situation and you certainly don't know anything about our scandals."

"I'm sorry," he said. "Don't be mad. I shouldn't have laughed at you. I was being rude."

This was better. "It's true," I said. "She's going to have a baby." Maybe he found my use of the phrase, *with child*, amusing. Maybe it was. I had never used it before.

"I don't think so," Jules said.

"Why do you say that?" I asked.

"I've talked to Sophie," Jules said.

"You talked to her about the baby?"

"No, we've never talked about the possibility of a baby," Jules said.

"Then you don't know."

But I could tell by his smile that he thought he knew more than I did.

"We talked about men," Jules said.

"And what did she say?" I resented the fact that Sophie had already confided in Jules.

Jules shrugged. "She said what most young women say about men."

I threw a fit and accused him of being treacherous. I accused him of lying to me and of not respecting my intellect. "I'm not stupid," I said.

"I'm sorry, Agnes," Jules said. "I don't want to make you mad, but I think you're wrong."

But I wasn't in the mood to hear his apologies. " You don't know everything in the world. You even admitted to me that you make up half the things you say."

"I know Sophie's not pregnant."

"How could you?" Even as I yelled at him, I knew he was right. Sophie wasn't going to have a baby.

"I know because she's admitted to me that she's a bit naïve when it comes to men."

I didn't know what that meant so I walked ahead and almost ran into a man on a bicycle. The man was old and had poor balance. He had his shopping in the back panniers and when he swerved to avoid hitting me, the bags of fruits and vegetables tipped out. I covered my face, afraid to watch as the tomatoes and green beans spilled onto the cobblestones.

Jules helped him regain his balance, apologizing for my clumsiness. I felt young and stupid and would have walked towards the street to take a bus home, but that would have meant walking straight uphill in the midday sun.

I was resentful because of the way Jules understood Sophie better than I did. I was her sister and yet I had no notion as to the truth of the situation that had brought us to the South of France.

Jules came over to me. "Let's go have ourselves a drink." He took me by the hand and walked me to the end of the flower market. We found a table outside the brasserie near the old church.

Jules ordered us crème de menthes. They were bright green and the glass pitcher of water was inlaid with flowers.

"Let's not talk anymore about Sophie," Jules said.

Fine, I thought. We don't have to talk at all.

My sabotage had somehow worked against me and I was unhappy and couldn't help but pout. I was too stupid, too naïve, too childish for a man of such sophistication. I closed my eyes, the heat of my tears pressing against my lids.

"Friends?" Jules asked. It seemed silly to be angry with my only friend on the Riviera. I nodded and whispered yes.

Jules poured out our drinks and I watched him stir his glass with a long spoon, then did exactly the same.

Jules held up his glass. "To us. To our happiness. Because that's what matters."

I raised my glass and did my best to seem carefree and good-natured, but didn't feel that way inside or out. I had borrowed one of Sophie's skirts. The waistband was too big and I had folded it over and pinned it, so instead of the material flouncing around my knees as it did on Sophie, it hung too heavy and too wide for my smaller frame.

Jules took a drink. "It's wonderful, isn't it?"

I was still crying. Just a bit and I'm not sure he saw my tears. If he did he didn't tell me not to cry, which was what Sophie would have done.

"You've told me a secret and now I'll tell you one," Jules said.

"A secret?" I asked and the terrible frustration and confusion I had been feeling drained from me. Just like that, it was gone. Somehow Jules had understood what I felt. He was the first person I had told about the scandal, the first person to hear how I had understood our reasons for being there and I wanted my revelation to matter to him. I wanted him to know that I had lost my mother, that I was lonely, that I loved my father, but he didn't seem to care too much for me. I wanted him to see the awfulness of Grandfather and the secrets that seemed to rule our family.

"Yes," Jules said. "A confidence. Something I would prefer you didn't tell anyone else." He sat back and put his hands in his pockets, looking around to see if anyone was hearing our conversation. We were quite alone.

"Who's it about?" I asked.

"Are secrets always about someone?" He smiled and looked surprised as if my talk was engaging him.

"Yes," I said. "The best kind of secrets are always about other people."

He considered this for several minutes. He finished his drink. His lips were stained a light green color from the menthe. "Then this is about me."

I thought he was going to tell me he was married and I dreaded hearing these words so much that I held my breath.

But he said nothing about a wife. Instead he talked about

Matisse, a name I knew, but whose work I could not bring to mind. "I am devoted to Henri Matisse. Like an apostle following the Lord, I am in awe of his wisdom. I am humbled by his talent."

The words poured out of him.

"The Greeks said our greatest virtue was passion and that's what I feel for Matisse," Jules finished.

That afternoon we made our first visit to Vence where I was to see passion. Vence was a medieval village with very narrow cobblestone streets and even narrower sidewalks. It looked like a dollhouse village, with pretend stores, a pretend post office, and pretend cypress trees. Olive groves surrounded the entrance into the village adding even more to its sense of a place out of time.

"This is where he lives," Jules said. We had parked the car outside the gates of La Rêve. "Isn't that perfect?" Jules asked. "Matisse came here during the war. To be safe. Others considered it best that he leave the country, but Matisse said he could not abandon France."

Later, to finish my education, Jules took me to a men's sports bar on a road just outside of Nice. The walls were covered with newspaper clippings. Large black and white photographs scotch-taped below long articles from the sporting newspapers. Most were of previous Tour de France winners. There, over a glass of panache, Jules revealed to me his obsession with Fausto Coppi.

"I thought it was Matisse."

"A man can bow to more than one deity," Jules said.

I never knew anyone who bowed to one, let alone two.

"There he is," Jules said. He pointed to the grainy black-and-white photograph. The man wore a tight-fitting cap with a wide brim that covered most everything on his face except his wide grin.

Jules explained that in 1949 Fausto Coppi had won the Giro d'Italia then two months later went on to win the Tour de France, the first man ever to win both in the same year. His victories were celebrated in both France and Italy and his reputation as a premiere athlete soared. It was then that the world began to refer to him as *el Campionissimo*, the greatest champion. The champion of all champions. The newspapers referred to him as "the idol of the masses."

Everyone in Italy was in love with him. Men and women. Gender made no difference.

Jules told me that bicycle racing had changed dramatically since the war. Or rather the people's appreciation of bicycling had changed. For the six years of the war, there were almost no sporting events. Nothing except the war. But things had changed. People wanted to restart. They wanted to have fun, to enjoy life again. They embraced sports, especially those where their own country-men excelled. Cycling became the pride of France, Italy, England, Belgium, and Spain. The good riders were treated like celebrities in cultures where individual achievements were not normally glorified.

It also helped that the minister of France decided to impose mandatory annual vacation time. With leisure time and a strong sense of national pride, most of the citizens rallied around their races and cheered on their rides. They poured out into the streets filled with the sense of a new beginning. "The tifosi," Jules explained. "The crazy Italian fans who will do anything for their hero."

What could I do but nod that I understood?

"My life has been dominated by these two giants. I live in the shadow of their genius."

I had never heard someone talk so passionately about anything before and I was transfixed. I loved him even more than I had when we set out that morning. The day was magical and I felt like I was floating above the earth. I no longer wanted to sabotage my sister. I no longer wanted to hurt anyone. I wanted to love like Jules did. I wanted to be engulfed as he was in adoration and respect.

"So now you know," Jules said. "Those are the secrets of my soul. The reason of my heart."

It took me a minute to speak. I strained to keep the tears out of my voice. "I think it's beautiful," I sighed.

"It is, isn't it?" Jules said. "I've never considered it like that, but you're right, Agnes: adoration is beautiful."

I was impressed, but more importantly I was in love.

"So that's my goal," Jules said.

"To meet them?" I asked.

"To be them," Jules said.

"But that's impossible," I said.

"I didn't say it would be easy, I said it's what I would like to achieve," Jules said. "I want to be as great as these men."

I sipped my drink, the bubbles gathered in my nose. "Have you told Sophie?"

"Oh no."

"No?" I asked.

"Absolutely not," Jules said. "She wouldn't understand."

My chest swelled with pride. He had said exactly the right thing. I was different. "You're right," I said. "She definitely wouldn't understand."

"But you can, can't you?" You can appreciate my love for these men," he told me.

"I can," I whispered. "But tell me why do you care so much about them?"

"Because they embody everything I want in life," Jules said. "I think our hearts' compasses are pointed in the same direction. We appreciate life in the same way."

"You do?"

"I think we do," Jules said. "Like Matisse, I concentrate on beauty. Like him, I ignore all that is ugly or distasteful."

"And Coppi?"

"Because he is simply the best at what he does."

This was my first lesson on Coppi and Matisse. My head was spinning. My heart, for perhaps the first time in my life, was full.

That night when Sophie asked me about the day I said something vague about the flower market in Nice.

She wrinkled her nose. Nice was one of her least favorite places on the Riviera. She thought it was an old port city with dingy dark streets and old smelly buildings. Old Russians, old Parisians, old tourists filled the narrow roads. The grand Promenade des Anglais on the seashore was not to her liking. "Look at all these old people," she said. "Walking. Walking. Walking. Where are they going? I'll tell you. They're marching towards death."

"It was wonderful," I said, careful not to tell her too much. Wonderful was an insufficient description to explain the best day of my life. I sighed and she asked if I was tired.

"Not at all," I whispered.

Grandfather had gone to bed. Sophie and I sat on the back patio. The evening light was gray. I could not see her face, only the glow of her cigarette.

There was something I needed to understand. "Are you going to have a baby?" I asked bluntly.

"Of course I'm not going to have a baby. Who put that notion in your head?" She puffed on her cigarette, the orange color deepened, I heard the sharp exhale of breath. "And lower your voice. Imagine if Grandfather heard that. He'd fly out the window in such a rage."

"If you're not pregnant, why did we come here?" I asked. "Why did we have to leave Paris?"

"Oh, I see," Sophie said. She shifted her weight in her chair.

"Will you ever tell me what happened?"

She sighed. "It must seem odd to you." She kicked off her sandals, and I heard the soft noise as she flicked them across the bricks.

"Will you tell me?"

"I can tell you it was complicated," Sophie said. She sighed again.

"But not the reason?"

She pulled her chair across the patio and sat across from me. She put her feet on my chair. Her toenails brushed against my skin. She had painted them red that afternoon and I worried that the polish had not dried sufficiently. I imagined red streaks running down my shins.

"The war made everything so complicated."

I laughed because she sounded so much like Father, who used the war to explain and define everything.

"I said the war was complicated. I didn't say it was amusing," Sophie said.

"Millions of Parisians lived through the war," I pointed out.

"Not all of them moved to their family vacation homes in the South of France. In fact, as far as I know, we were the only ones."

"I'm sure some did," Sophie said. "I'm sure some did exactly as we have done."

"I won't argue the count," I said. "I'd like you to tell me the truth, but if you're not going to, then tell me you're not going to. Please don't ramble on about the war and how complicated those years were."

"Father hasn't been happy," she said. "Not in a long time."

"So he got rid of his family?"

"More or less."

"He called the reason we left a scandal," I said. "I'd say it had to do with something much more than simple unhappiness."

"Father was miserable. Mother's death was terrible for him. I think he felt that without her his family was half formed. We were continually reminders that there was something missing in his life. Do you notice how he rarely writes? How we so rarely hear from him?"

"Is that the real reason?" I asked. It didn't ring true. It didn't sound like Sophie was talking about our family.

"Not exactly," Sophie said. "But it sounds tragic, doesn't it?"

The church in Menton rang the bells of the hour. Ten bells. The sun was exhausting and I was always tired at nightfall. I stood and kissed Sophie good-night. I decided that she was in the dark just as much as I was. She had no idea what the scandal was. It no longer mattered why we had been sent away. What mattered now was that we never leave. Scandal or not, I now worried that Father would change his mind. I worried that as quickly as we had been sent down, we would be sent back to Paris. Now that I knew Jules, I never wanted to leave. I wanted to live on the Riviera forever.

Chapter Four

Sophie wasted no time going after her goal. Like a true competitor, she was organized, very meticulous, and extremely bossy. She had no qualms telling Jules and I what she wanted done every day.

One idea of hers was to find a man at the Nice airport.

"There are men everywhere on the Riviera," Jules said. "Why isolate our search to the airport?"

"I'm looking for sophisticated and wealthy," she explained. She perused the airplane arrival notices, which were printed in *Nice-Matin* two or three times a week. The passenger lists of all incoming flights were listed along with a grand welcome to the Riviera. In 1951, air travel was limited to the rich, and flying into Nice was for the extremely rich. Everyone else came by train. Sophie went through the lists carefully trying to decide who had money, who was single, who was a French citizen, who was living abroad, what their business was in the area.

Jules admired her skill in deciphering the names on the lists. "The Allies could have used someone like you."

"I need to find someone important," Sophie said. "I'd like a man of some importance."

"Or at least rich," Jules said.

"Aren't all rich people important?" Sophie asked.

"I don't know many rich people," Jules said and shrugged.

"Trust me," Sophie said.

"I have no choice but to trust you, darling," Jules said.

The passenger lists included the names of those flying as well as their home cities and addresses of where they would be staying in the South of France; often, there was word or two about their profession: *Artist, businessman, designer.*

"Jules Agard," I said. "*Resident of the Riviera.*" I recalled how he had introduced himself to us that afternoon in Monte Carlo.

"Artist of not much talent. I prefer to be called a man of leisure." Jules said. "Jules Agard. A professional man of leisure."

She circled names. "If they're good-looking, we'll move on to step two," she said.

Jules and I had to be with her. "I can't go by myself," she said. "A woman alone in an airport. No. No. No."

"But won't a man find your entourage intimidating?" I asked.

"You're my decoys," she said. "I'll use you if I need to."

To her credit, there was something thrilling about seeing the gigantic planes drop out of the clouds.

The city of Nice built the airport on an old dump. No one told the sea gulls that their home was being destroyed and they returned just as they did every year. Thousands of them came back. The sea gulls were grouped in a large, solid-looking mass. From where we stood, it looked more like a gigantic white sheet had been draped over the runway.

They cried out—one long sound—that carried across the water. A powerful breeze blew across the tarmac, and their bodies undulated. The movement was a ripple, like a flag waving in the afternoon sun. And then the sound of a plane came and they scattered—a thick fog lifting all at once. It was magical.

*L*ike the sea gulls, we returned. Often.

One day, we saw someone we knew. "Mademoiselle. Mademoiselle," a voice called to us. I looked up.

"How's your Grandfather?" It was Grandfather's new eye doctor.

"As well as can be expected," I said. "As usual, he complains."

"About his eyesight?"

"About everything," I said. "He doesn't limit his unhappiness to his failing vision."

"Give him my best," the doctor said.

"He's looking forward to his next appointment," I said. "He likes that you pay him so much attention."

"And I look forward to seeing him again."

"I find that hard to believe," I said. We had joked like that when I took Grandfather to his office his last time there. He smiled and nodded goodbye.

He left. Sophie waited until he was halfway across the tarmac before pushing her hands into my thighs. "Who was that man?"

I thought our conversation had made his identification perfectly clear.

"Grandfather's doctor is ancient. He had wrinkly skin and his teeth are yellow."

"That one had a heart attack," I said. Sophie had conned me into going the last two visits.

"When?"

I shrugged. I had heard the whole story during our last visit. The receptionist told it over and over every time a new patient came in for their appointment. She called it "fortunate" that it had been after hours and only the cranky receptionist had been there. She was the one who heard his cry, then his fall from the next room. When she went in—it was too late—he was dead.

"That was his grandson."

"His grandson?"

I asked her how long she was going to repeat everything I said.

"Until I start getting answers that satisfy my questions."

"That man is in charge of the practice now, " I said.

"He's got a medical degree?" Sophie asked.

"He didn't show it to me," I said. "But he seems to know what he's doing. If he's a fake, Grandfather didn't notice."

"Well, I'll be," Sophie said.

"He's very funny," I said. "I haven't the slightest idea if he knows anything about eyes."

It was noon. The sun directly overhead was fierce. The airport was the worst place to be midday and I said something about wasting our time. "We could be on the beach."

Sophie was at once understanding and sympathetic to my discomfort.

"It is hot," she said. "Oh dear, I feel like such a bother."

"It's about time you realized it," I said, though it wasn't gratifying being mean when she was suddenly so nice. Where was the fun if she was going to understand how boring it was at the airport?

"Do you find this dull, Jules?"

It was not like Sophie to inquire about others' boredom.

Jules shrugged. "For you, darling, I'll do anything."

"Why don't you two go on ahead," Sophie said.

"And just forget about the plane?" I asked. "You're going to let one go? What if the man of your dreams is on it?"

"I'm going to wait," Sophie said. "But you two don't have to waste your time here."

"Fine," I said. "Let's go, Jules."

Jules protested, but I insisted we take advantage of our freedom. It was hot and the plane was late. There was no telling when or even if it would arrive.

We got into the car.

"Cap Ferrat?" I asked. I had my bathing suit in my bag.

"Vence," Jules insisted. "Unless you're tired of it."

Our second trip that week, but I had no reason to protest.

The winds were strong and we drove away from the coast and into the hills above Cannes as if late for an agreed appointment—as if a meeting with Matisse was imminent.

I put off going home as long as I could. We stopped in Nice and had a coffee at a bistro there. I asked Jules if he wanted to take a walk along the Pier. The sun was low in the sky, clouds had gathered at the horizon. Rain threatened. I loved being on the coast when a storm came across the mountains and went out to sea. I thought it would be romantic to walk away from the shores just as the wind was gathering force, the rain clouds moving swiftly overhead. I had heard that there were fortune-tellers who came out at night—Russian women with powers to see beyond the present, and I was anxious to see what one of them might see in my life.

"It's late," he said. "I should get you home."

"Are you busy?" We did not talk about what he did when we were not together. It had occurred to me that he might have a secret girlfriend, one who he only saw at night. I burned with jealousy for this imaginary girl. "Of course you're busy. You probably have a thousand things to do tonight."

"I'm not as interesting as all that," Jules said.

But I thought of Jules as wildly exciting. I imagined him dancing at nightclubs, walking along the boardwalk with a huge following of friends and admirers. I saw him in Nice at the corner bars, eating, drinking, and talking, until all hours of the morning. I imagined him listening to music, walking the narrow dark streets near dawn, coming down to the beach to see the sunrise. I saw him taking his girlfriend, the one I had imagined for him. I thought of her as blond, curvy, loud—the exact opposite of me. They would wander to the harbor where they would sit and watch the ships as they readied to journey to Corsica and to other ports of call far beyond the south of France.

"Can we ever go to your place?" I asked him as we drove up the mountains towards home.

"I don't think that would be appropriate," he said.

"Why not?"

"A young woman like you visiting a man's apartment?" Jules spun the steering wheel as we approached the Villa. "I hardly think your father would approve of that."

His talk was flirtatious. It insinuated that there was something sexual in our relationship. I was thrilled and forgot all about the curvy, breathy blonde.

He drove the car onto the gravel, the tires welcoming it. "The house looks empty. Are you sure you're going to be okay?" He nodded towards the Villa, which was sitting in darkness. The shutters along the front side were closed tight, though it was too early for them to be shut for the night.

"Probably because of the rain," I said. "Mathilde is afraid of thunderstorms."

"I thought she was afraid of bees."

Sophie and I had told him about Mathilde's fears.

"Her fears are not limited to insects." Mathilde's list of phobias was extensive: bees, dragonflies, trains, hedgehogs, hurricanes, bats, the old woman who sold vegetables at the local market. She was afraid of Grandfather; she wasn't that comfortable with Cook. She feared loud noises and told me that only people with no brains flew in airplanes. Mathilde told Sophie she no longer wanted to do any work on the second floor of the Villa. She claimed it was haunted.

"I don't care for ghosts," Jules said.

"Neither does Mathilde," I said. I didn't talk much about life at the Villa with Jules. I thought our domestic scene incredibly tiresome and worried that he would find it even duller than I did. He wasn't like other adults. He didn't ask about trivial matters. When he spoke, he spoke of cycling or Matisse's art. We talked on a very sophisticated level—art and ideas. Desire. We did not bother with the quotidian.

"Spirits and ghosts belong to the past. It's gone. Over and done with. I'm not even that fond of memories."

I knew what he meant. I had a hard time remembering my mother and when I did I found that I couldn't bring any images of her to mind. I could see the dark hallways, the sheets, a blue shawl that she used to drape around her shoulders. I could smell camphor. I remembered the glass by the side of her bed—the way it had been marked by fingerprints—but I could no longer see her. Her face, her body, her very image were no longer mine.

I once told Jules some details of my mother's death and he dismissed them as if they were bothersome. "Let's not talk about that," Jules said. "It will only depress us." At the time it had surprised me but now that I knew him, I felt in accordance. It was a relief to be around an adult who did not talk of the dead, of the war, of the suffering, and of things that belong to another time. It was exciting to talk only of what we *would* do and not what we could have done.

"The present is the only thing worth caring about," Jules said.

I knew this was not how most people felt. Grandfather did nothing but talk about the past. He didn't believe in a future though I told him that each time the sun came up, it showed how wrong he was.

"That's exactly right," I said. "The present is the only thing that one should worry about. The past is past. It's gone."

It was refreshing to think that way. Erasing the past meant doing away with remorse, with regret, with sadness. There was something exuberant about the future—as if we were running headlong into sunlight—warm days, soft breezes, and the air smelling of the sea. It was the magic of tomorrow and I embraced it as I knew Jules did.

"Our souls are in agreement," Jules said. "We think alike."

"Our hearts too," I whispered. I wanted him to know how I felt, but I was much too timid to admit my desire. I vowed that I would wait for him.

"What's that, little one?" Jules asked.

I just smiled and told him again that I agreed with the way he saw the world.

*T*he house was absolutely still. It was the first time I had ever come home and found the place in darkness. The thick vines that surrounded the walls of the property made the Villa seem darker than it really was.

Grandfather's absence was especially surprising. Except for visits to the doctor's, Grandfather had no reason or desire to leave the Villa. In the distance, I heard the thunder approaching.

The kitchen was empty or so I thought until I saw Mathilde. She was sitting at the table with her embroidery basket. She had carried over a lamp and tilted the shade so that the white light shone directly on the material she was working on. She acknowledged my presence with a slight nod of her head. One of the strangest things about the villa was the wood table in the kitchen. It was enormous, much too big for the room. Too wide to fit through the doorframe or the windows, Sophie joked that the villa must have been built around the table. I imagined one of my relatives, someone I had never met, building it in the room.

"Has Sophie been home?"

She bent her head closer to her material. I went over and pushed open the shutters. Large raindrops fell slowly from the sky. The air smelled of fruit and flowers.

"It's going to storm," Mathilde finally spoke.

A crack of thunder echoed across the mountain, and then the rain came down in droves.

"Where's Grandfather?" I asked. "Are he and Sophie together?"

I figured Cook was at the house down the road. She had become friendly with the woman who worked down there and they spent time together, especially in the early evenings.

"Not a word when others are about, then suddenly all these questions," Mathilde said smugly.

I seesawed on my feelings for Mathilde. She was such a strange quirky creature, whose obvious dislike of her living situation must have made her days miserable. Some days I felt sorry for her; other days I didn't think of her at all. But I no longer teased her like I used to. Oddly, though, she didn't seem to notice the change in my behavior.

"Mathilde," I said, trying to be nice. "Could you please tell me where everyone is?"

Mathilde would not let anything be that easy. She finished a row of stitches then, just as I was about to leave the kitchen, said something about having no idea as to Sophie's whereabouts.

I went over and cut off some cheese. I ate it standing there by the cutting board. Mathilde scolded me. "The mice will have a field day."

"Sorry," I said and leaned over the sink to finish a second piece. I washed my hands, and dried them on the back of my skirt.

"Your Grandfather is visiting a friend," Mathilde said. The room was filled with night shadows from the odd position of the light. Our bodies on the far wall looked gigantic.

"Who?" I asked. "Where did he go?"

"A woman," Mathilde explained. "Someone he knew from the past. From years ago."

I had never heard of anything so surprising.

"Why should that be a surprise? Shouldn't he have friends?" she asked. "Isn't he allowed to have friends?"

She was suddenly so animated and loud, I wondered if she hadn't been drinking.

"It's not a question of should or shouldn't, he just doesn't," I answered.

Even in Paris, Grandfather did not have friends. He left the house but walked down to the park and spent the day with men there. I don't think he considered them anything more than acquaintances. He never talked of friends or of visiting people. He didn't make lunch dates. He never went out at night.

"Well, now he does," Mathilde said.

Mathilde studied her embroidery very closely, then looked up at me as if something had just occurred to her. "What do you do all day?" she asked. "When you go off in that fancy car, where do you go?"

I hoped she wasn't going to ask if she could come along. I hesitated, but finally thought it rude not to answer her question. "Mostly we go to the beach or to the promenades in Nice or Monte Carlo. Sometimes we go other places. Why?"

"Do you put your body in the surf?" she asked. Instead of the scissors, she used her teeth to cut the thread. She was very quick. She spit the tiny pieces of thread out, turning her head so they would not soil what she was working on.

"Sometimes," I said.

"I'd be afraid," she told me.

"Of the ocean?" I asked. "Why? It's lovely. So warm and blue and so clear you can see the fish swimming about." The sea was one of my favorite things.

"Where I come from, the ocean is very rough and cold."

"Because it's in the north," I interrupted.

She made a perfect O with her mouth, then spoke softly. "I never realized you were familiar with my part of the country."

"I'm not," I said. "But I know where Normandy is on the map. I know it's cold up there."

"As I was saying, no one bathes in the surf. Maybe a few crazy people wade in during the warmest months, but the people with brains in their head stay away."

I had heard this story before. I had discovered in my fifteen years on the planet that most everyone had one story they wanted to tell over and over. Something happened in their youth, which somehow defined them. Grandfather talked about his first experience riding the underground in Paris. My Aunt Cecille's was about losing her purse in a Paris restaurant and the waiter, who returned it, told her she was the most beautiful woman he had ever seen. She told that story to everyone—even to her husband. Mathilde's story was about a man who she saw drown in the Atlantic Ocean.

"I saw him. He struggled with the sea. The currents were strong," Mathilde said. "It was in May. The waters must have been freezing. It was hard to know if he drowned in the waves or if he simply froze in the icy waters. Had he just decided to go swimming when the water temperature and the force of the waves overwhelmed him, or was it deliberate?"

I didn't understand why if everyone in the village had witnessed the act, no one had done anything to help the poor man. It was a detail she never fully explained.

"My guess is he did both," I said.

"Did you know him?" Mathilde said. She pulled the light closer to the edge of the table. Light spilled into the room.

I laughed. She could be so funny, even when she wasn't trying to be.

"I don't think I knew him, Mathilde."

"Then I guess my next question is, how would you know?"

"I'm talking about scientifically that's what would happen to a body. The water would cause the body to go into hypothermia and the person would basically faint and then without help they'd drown."

"You certainly know a lot for a girl who's never seen a man drown."

I wanted my bath. But the idea of walking upstairs in the dark was not inviting. I didn't believe in ghosts, but a dark empty house was spooky.

"What are you making?" I asked and reached for the cloth she held in her hands. It was square, an off-white color, with tiny lace at the corners.

"They're napkins."

"Why do you have so many?"

"They're for my trousseau."

It was a word I had not heard very often and I was surprised to hear it from Mathilde.

"Are you getting married?" I asked.

"Certainly," she said.

"You are?" It was the first I had heard of a man in Mathilde's life. I was taken aback and couldn't help but stare. To think that she had kept her upcoming nuptials a secret was astonishing.

"Of course," she said. "Poor girls do marry, you know."

I rolled my eyes. Her logic never made sense. I had never insinuated that she shouldn't marry. I was simply surprised to learn that there were plans underway.

Mathilde had days off—two half days a week—but I never knew what she did with her time. I had never seen anyone come for her.

More importantly, I had never heard any gossip or teasing from Cook about an intended for Mathilde.

"When?" I demanded to know. Was it someone from the Riviera? Had she just met someone? Did Sophie know all this?

"Someday," she said. "Someday I'm going to be married."

"Do you know the man you're going to marry?" I asked.

"Not yet," she said and shrugged as if I was naming an unimportant detail of the whole marriage thing. "I'll certainly know him before we marry."

The rain drummed on the roof.

"Then how do you know it will happen? What if you never fall in love?"

"I know I will," she said. She spoke of marriage in the same way Sophie did. There was no trace of longing, no wistful sighs, no self-doubt—just simple conviction that one day a man would come into their lives and they would marry him.

"But if you haven't even met him yet, why do all this work?"

"Because when I do meet him, I want to be ready." She clicked the trigger on the embroidery hoop and the two pieces came apart. She pulled the material taut, then folded it and set it in the basket. She cleaned up the rest of her threads and wiped the table of any remains.

I was overwhelmed by the futility of her work. If someone like Sophie was struggling to find a husband, how would Mathilde ever think she would find one? Sophie was beautiful and fun, Mathilde just the opposite. Men didn't want women like Mathilde. It made me feel awful.

I fingered the soft lace circles, the cotton sheets, and the piles of cloth napkins. I felt sorry for her, but hated my snobbish attitude. But there it was. It was how I felt about the situation. Rather than speak about it though, I told her another truth. "It's really beautiful. Your husband will be most impressed."

"Thank you," she said and I knew that she was very pleased. Pleased by her work and pleased that I had noticed how beautiful the work was.

I saw her years of hard work stored away in an attic, dusty and forgotten, a waste of time. I saw the clean white material turning yellow with the passing years. The careful stitches being chewed away by rodents or moths making their home in the woolen blankets.

No longer caring if it was dark, I went up to my room and shut the door. I sat on the bed and waited for Sophie, but fell asleep before she came home.

Chapter Five

Sophie was suddenly under the weather. Too sick to get out of bed, she encouraged me to go off with Jules on my own. "You don't mind, do you, sweetie?" she asked.

"What's to mind?" I asked. "If you're sick, you're sick."

"And I am," she said. "But that's no reason to spoil your good time. You can have fun without me, can't you?"

It was exactly what I wanted but not being used to getting my way, I hesitated.

"Go," she directed. "Careful of the sun. Wear your hat. Especially if you're going to spend all the day on the beach."

I appreciated her being so nice and asked if I could get her anything.

"I'm fine," Sophie said. And she seemed to be—the least sick person I had ever seen.

I worried that Jules would be disappointed when he learned that Sophie wouldn't be joining us for awhile. I worried that I wasn't charming or interesting. That I wasn't pretty enough or sophisticated enough, or simply that I was too young. But Jules didn't seem concerned with Sophie's absence. He asked after her health, then started the car's engine and drove down the mountain. "We mustn't waste our day up here doing nothing," he said.

Both pleased and surprised by his attention, I put my faith in the hope that he was falling in love with me.

Without Sophie, we were free. There were no more boring afternoons at the airport. We went to Vence. We kept track of the bicycle races.

Two days later, Jules took me north of San Remo where the Giro d'Italia was to pass through. The Giro d'Italia was a three week bicycle race—over twenty day stages. It was the most important bicycle race in their country—it rivaled the Tour de France.

"You must see the great man for yourself," Jules said.

We left Menton before dawn. Grandfather had not given me permission to be away the whole day, but I had not asked for it either. He would not have approved of me crossing the border with Jules. He would not have believed the story of wanting to see an Italian bicyclist. I asked Jules to meet me at the crossroads so that no one would hear the crunch of his car tires on the stones in the driveway. The clandestine nature of my departure gave the day a stolen quality, an adventure out of time, a day I never wanted to see end.

I was early. Jules was surprisingly late.

Jules had overslept and cursed himself for his tardiness. "A lazy stupid man," he said. "If we miss Coppi, I shall never forgive myself. Never."

Jules' dramatic nature made me laugh, which he said was not appropriate behavior for such a monumental day.

"Will it really be that wonderful?" I asked.

"Of course," Jules said. "We'll be in the presence of the greatest bicycle rider in the world. What more could one want?"

We drove like mad—racers inspired by what we were going to witness. We had several maps on the seat beside us, but as there was only one motor route that close to the coastline, I shoved them under the car seat and watched Jules who drove with concentration and determination.

Jules and I arrived hours before the racers were scheduled to come through—but we were hardly the only ones there.

"The tifosi," Jules explained. "The crazy Italian fans." He looked on with disapproval, as if he had imagined we'd be alone when Coppi rode past. "They're fanatical."

The people seemed to have come from everywhere, as if the earth itself had suddenly opened and was pouring people towards the narrow road. Men in boots with mud from the day's labor came, women who dressed as their mothers had dressed fifty years before, long dark skirts, aprons, hair bonnets. Dozens and dozens of children, some in costume, others with Italian flags. They brought food and beer and made open fires where they roasted meat all morning long.

The mood of the day was infectious. The exuberance of what was to come, thrilling.

"They say that the blood in his veins has been replaced with petrol."

"That sounds horrible."

"It's a metaphor," Jules said. "To explain why he can ride so fast."

"Just as long as it's not the truth."

In the mountains the temperature was dramatically different than on the coast. Fog hung on the horizon and from where we stood we could see patches of snow surrounding the peaks above us.

The crowds had been there all morning, drinking beer, cooking sausages, singing, dancing, painting names of the riders on the road with orange, white, and green paints. The shouts and screaming were in Italian, but it wasn't difficult to understand what people were saying. We watched, but then caught up in the exuberance, joined in. We sang songs we didn't know the words to, imitated the cries of the people next to us, accepted bottles of beer and drank from them, before passing them on to our neighbors.

The afternoon in the Italian mountains was a carnival, a great celebration of national pride, or joy that in a few hours hundreds of bicyclists would come storming down from the mountains—one of them the national hero. It was like nothing I had ever experienced—even at the end of the war—the Germans leaving Paris. Then I had been happy that others were happy, but childish in that I didn't understand why we were shouting and crying for joy.

Then just when the party atmosphere seemed as if it would

wane, a buzz went through the crowds: "They're coming. They're coming. They're going to be here soon!" The words passed like a telegraph service of spectators that the racers were on their way. Here was the reason we had come here. Here was our purpose.

The sponsor vehicles came first. One after another, a parade of cars with signs advertising the teams and their products. They were brightly colored and honked as they made their way down from the mountains.

Silence descended on the onlookers.

"There," Jules said. "Look."

He need not have told me where to look. Everyone around us turned, a wave of movement all directed at one rider.

"It's him. It's him," the cheers went up.

But it wasn't.

It was a kid who had jumped onto the course and waved as he pedaled past. The crowds booed and chased him until he veered off the road and hit one of the barricades that separated the spectators from the riders.

I moved closer to Jules. He put his arm around my shoulder. "You can see, can't you?"

Jules was sweating with excitement. I put my head close to his shoulder and was actually touching his skin. It smelled of hair tonic and peppermint. I closed my eyes and breathed deeply.

Jules leaned down and whispered in my ear. "He'll be here."

I thought I would swoon when his breath moved across my shoulder blades.

Jules grabbed my hand. "I think it's him."

And there he was. Two riders coming towards us. Two riders pedaling side by side. One was Coppi, the other a teammate.

Coppi raced for *Team Bianchi* and the name of the team was stitched across his chest and down the side of his shorts. He wore white socks and a tight white cap, with large aviator glasses that made him look like a giant insect. He had deflated bicycle tubes around his chest that made him look as if he were carrying a pack. He had bottles of water in the back of his shirt, a fast-moving camel.

Two seconds in coming, half a second in passing and then whoosh, he was gone.

Jules was speechless as Coppi approached.

I jumped up and down screaming.

And what happened next happened so quickly, it was hard to think of it as real. A man, overcome with emotion or alcohol, jumped over the knee-high barricade and chased Coppi along the sharp upgrade. "I love you. I love you," he shouted. Coppi had slowed to take a drink of water. He was slack-jawed and his face wind-beaten. He did not turn when the man called his name—not even when the man screamed at the top of his voice. Frustrated and angry at being ignored by his hero, the man reached out and grabbed Coppi's shirt.

Everything quieted at once—it was a moment suspended in time. Most of us, thought Coppi was going to be pulled off. It seemed inevitable. He struggled to stay on the bike. His feet were in these clips wrapped around the pedals and he used his arms to keep steady. There was a collective gasp as we waited for the champion to fall to the pavement. His teammate was struck dumb and motionless as everyone waited to see what would happen next.

Coppi and the drunk man were now connected, Coppi dragged him up the hill, pulling with all his might. The team cars had not come around or one of them could have knocked the guy off.

Jules gasped when he saw that the man meant to pull the great Coppi down. "It can't happen. It's not possible," he said. "It's just not possible."

Jules stepped over the barricade and jumped on the road, onto the course. He sprinted after the man who was holding onto Coppi. Coppi, still engaged in the struggle, was pulling with all his might, dragging the man behind him.

Jules acted quickly. He ran and caught the man, then with all his might, overpowered him and pulled him to the ground. Coppi, freed at last, burst forward with a huge surge of energy. Jules and the drunk man rolled into the gutter.

Jules stood, the man up on all fours like a dog stayed with his head on the ground.

There were more cars. Honking. Shouting, yelling, mayhem closing in and I worried that Jules would get run over. The motorcycles, the team cars, a rush of vehicles and pretty soon, I lost sight of him.

Then the peloton came through. The peloton was the pack, the major group of riders. They rode together because it was easier to work off someone, to draft behind another's tire. Soon a few would break ahead and try to catch Coppi, but at the time, most were struggling just to stay with the group. It was a giant whoosh of tires on the road, wheels spinning, men breathing, a pack of determination beating down to the finish line.

To compensate for the cooler temperatures so far above sea level, the cyclists stuffed newspapers into their jerseys, which could easily be discarded. With no more use of wind and cold protection, and not wanting the extra weight, the men now got rid of the newspapers en masse. For several minutes it looked like it was raining newspaper. Kids went crazy trying to gather up as many as they could.

Jules was standing just off the road, a bit dazed. "Did you see?"

"You were wonderful," I said.

"It was wonderful," he corrected me.

"You were the only one who did anything," I started to explain why I was so impressed, but the tifosi wouldn't let us be.

We were too far away to see the finish, but we learned almost immediately that Coppi had won the day's race. He had crossed the finish line only a few seconds before the next man. The ground trembled and I thought the world might be coming to an end, but it was only the excitement of the crowds.

The entire town had been decorated with orange, green, and white ribbons. They hung from the lampposts and street signs. But the piazza had been given special attention, as this is where the award ceremony was to be held.

What followed was bedlam. One minute Jules and I were standing on a street corner, the next we were being carried by the crowds of people rushing to get close to the end of the race. Jules was stunned.

"Did you hurt yourself?" I asked.

He wiped his face with the same side of his handkerchief, making it worse. His cheeks were streaked with dirt.

The crowd carried us the entire two blocks until we were in the center of the village. We moved like a wave coming ashore until we finally ended up in the village piazza.

Coppi was in the center. He had taken off his hat and sunglasses and for the first time I saw his face.

The race officials moved him over to the makeshift podium where three girls in native costumes of lace and ribbons were standing with gigantic flower bouquets—tulips, roses, mimosas, and poinciana. Once beautiful, the bouquets had obviously spent the day outside. They were wilted, but Coppi accepted them with grace. He kissed the girls. They were timid and stared at their feet, as if afraid to look at the great racer.

One of the race officials made a speech, which I didn't understand. Afterwards he presented Coppi with a large silver emblem. Coppi kissed the mayor and the mayor's assistant. He had a large nose and wide grin. His mouth moved the entire time. We were not close enough to hear his words, not that we would have understood them. A three-man band stood ready to play a song from the region. Someone cued them and they began. The music was off-key, but enthusiastic; a few minutes later, it stopped. Coppi must have said something about Jules, because all of a sudden the men standing nearby grabbed Jules and lifted him onto the tabletop. "Here. Here," they said. "Here is your Frenchman."

Coppi nodded his appreciation. He called out across the piazza; everyone burst into applause and the men holding Jules' legs cheered as if Jules was a prize animal.

Jules looked over at Coppi and saluted. Later I asked him why he had made such a military gesture to his idol.

"To have run up and kissed his feet would have been impossible given my position," Jules said.

Coppi must have asked who had pulled off the wild fan and the crowd brought Jules to him. I was carried along as the friend of the man who had saved Coppi's win.

Coppi spoke in short bursts of breath and words. "You, my French friend," he said. "You have saved my life." He spoke French with a heavy accent, but we understood his words.

People were pressing in, trying to get closer. Fausto held out his arm and asked that they stand back. "A moment with this man," he said over and over. "Just a moment."

But the crowd couldn't back off. They were enthralled. They wanted their hero. They wanted the chance to adore him.

So Coppi simply leaned over and kissed Jules on both cheeks. "I will never forget what you did for me today, my friend. This I will remember in my heart."

The race officials moved him away and Jules stood alone in a shining moment of glory. The newspapermen and photographers suddenly circled around Jules. "Stand straight," they demanded. A man touched my shoulders and told me to move a bit to the right. I did.

We were herded into the local café. The windows were blocked out. Every inch of spare wall, and window space had been covered with newspaper clippings of past races. Photographs of Coppi and articles about him were everywhere.

With Coppi gone, the owner of the café and the men feted us like we were heroes. We were given plates of salami, cheese, and very hard bread. There were plates of olives, snails simmered in butter, plates full of salted herring, dishes of things I had never tasted, but did when they were passed, because someone was sure to protest if I didn't. We drank wine. We cheered ourselves. We cheered Coppi. We cheered Jules.

The Italians sang. Loud joyous songs, celebrating their country, the wonderful people who came from there. They were unabashedly exuberant about their victories.

The crowd continued its celebration long after Coppi's entourage got in their cars and drove away—the bicycle wheels tied to their roofs.

And even then, there was no silence. The owner turned on his radio and we listened as the sport's announcers from the large cities broadcast the day's win.

Every time San Remo was mentioned, the crowd started all over again with its cheering and applauding. If there were other riders in the Tour, the small village on the French border did not acknowledge them. Coppi would win the Tours. In July, the men predicted, he would ride into Paris, down the Champs-Élysées a winner.

At dusk, we headed back to Menton.

"My greatest regret is not to have been born Italian," Jules told me.

"I thought your greatest regret was not having been born Fausto Coppi."

"If I was Fausto Coppi, than I would already be Italian and would not have to worry about anything."

I knew what he meant about wanting to be Italian, about wanting to be more of a part of what we had just witnessed. The exuberance of the afternoon was seductive, and I longed for it to be the beginning of the day so that we could do it all over again, even though we had just left. I compared the jubilation of the Italians that afternoon to the somberness and silence of my house and the difference made me lonely.

"You wouldn't be overwhelmed with all the attention?" I asked.

"I would be proud to be admired like that," Jules said.

I tucked my legs up under myself and put my head back on the seat. I wanted to tell Jules I admired him like that, but didn't. I was pretty sure my romantic feelings were not reciprocated. Not just yet. But I had hope and that's what I was counting on. For now we were partners in our hero worship. I was a determined sort and thought that with enough patience and enough persistence, I would get what I wanted.

"You must learn to love him," Jules told me and I assured him that I would do my best. Jules was insistent. "You must learn to love him like I do."

"It's what you say about Matisse. I must learn to love him."

"That's right."

I knew the passion of a united heart.

The border guards waved us back into France without a glance. Italians, they had probably listened to the Tour on their transistor radios. They were tired from the celebrations of the day.

"Every day should be like today," Jules said. "They should all be this great."

The evening sky was a deep purple. Bats circled from the mountains. I could not see the sea, but the air smelled salty and cool. We moved quickly, turning and twisting as we drove back into France, back to familiar grounds. For once, Jules had spoken the truth; the day had been brilliant.

*W*e went on self-designed tours of Nice and Cimiez and Vence, retracing Matisse's life on the Riviera. We walked by the Hotel Beau Rivage on the Rue Saint-François de Paule, the one right behind the Quai des Etats Unis, the main boulevard that curves with the shore. This was where Matisse lived when he came to Nice as a young man. Jules showed me the paintings which had been painted from the balcony. Looking directly on the ocean, it must have been magical to open the doors to the blue waters.

"Matisse thinks the richness and silvery clarity of the light in Nice is quite unique and absolutely indispensable," Jules quoted Matisse from printed sources he had stored in a file box in the trunk of his car. "Matisse says that here on the Riviera, light plays the leading role in inspiring his work; color comes later."

"I know what he means," I said.

"Matisse said that if he had stayed up north in Paris, he never would have painted the kinds of things he did. His paintings would have been filled with browns, grays, fog, shading."

"It is a magical place," I agreed. "One feels that great things are possible here."

"Do you feel it too?" Jules asked.

"I do," I answered.

It was a honeymoon—at least what I imagined a honeymoon to be. Minus the romance and yet every other ingredient was there—

long hours when it was just the two of us, the warm sun, the beaches, the exotic people, the picnics in the woods, the long walks up and down the *Promenade des Anglais*. Our mad passionate love affair had yet to develop. I waited, but as the days passed, I began to worry that things weren't progressing.

Jules seemed content and happy. But he did not seem to be in love with me.

I blamed Jules' lack of interest in pursuing me on Fausto Coppi. More specifically, I blamed his lack of love on Coppi's poor showing in the Giro d'Italia. The *Campionissimo* was not at the top of his form and Jules grew more despondent with each of his stage losses. In the end, he did not have the strength or the luck to win the Giro.

We had stopped for a coffee at a small café in Monte Carlo and Jules listened to the race results on the radio with the men at the bar. I sat at a table on the sidewalk. The café was situated on a narrow cobblestone street.

"Even the best have bad races," I offered.

"He's had a terrible year," Jules said when he delivered the news of Coppi's loss. He came in fourth, not even earning a place on the podium. "This is a disaster. They must be mourning in the towns of Italy."

I could not imagine the crowds of people we saw cheering him on as anything but proud of their native son. "There's always next year," I said.

"I don't think anyone would be in favor of waiting an entire year. That's a very long time."

The sports announcers blamed his loss on his recovering from the broken collarbone he suffered in the Milan-Turin race. He fell in a race he had all but won, on his final lap in the velodrome riding towards his victory. He walked away from it then but was later taken to the hospital where the doctors told him that he had broken his collarbone.

"So maybe he wasn't at his best," I said. "Accidents are the cyclists' greatest enemies."

This was something Jules had told me. He didn't seem to notice that my statement wasn't original; he nodded in complete agreement. "That's right. That's right. But he's ready now. He'll win the Tour de France," Jules predicted and I was relieved to hear him express some optimism.

"Of course he will."

"The Tour de France is the greatest cycling feat in the world," Jules said. "No matter what the Italians claim. The Tour is a much more important race than anything that happens in their country."

"And he's sure to win," I said. "Maybe he's saving up his energy so that he can fly across the finish line, kilometers ahead of everybody else."

"You're a very quick study, Agnes," Jules said, and I basked in his praise.

But in the ninth stage of the 1950 Giro d'Italia en route from Venice to Bolzano, a rider in front of Coppi fell , for no apparent reason. There was no flat tire, the weather was dry, the winds were still. Coppi struggled to keep his balance, but couldn't. He went down hard and had to drop out of the race. He suffered a triple fracture of the pelvis and spent 29 days in bed. The entire season was lost.

No one wanted Coppi to win more than me. If Coppi were at the top of his form, Jules would be happy and then maybe he could stop worrying and pay me the attention I desired. I wanted him to court me. To woo me. It was time, I decided. It was time for Jules to declare his mad love for me.

Like the couple at the café across the cobblestone alley from where we were sitting. They were young lovers. Their embrace caught my attention. They were kissing, their arms entwined, their embrace desperate. I watched with envy—their passion was captivating—wishing I had the courage to blurt out my love to Jules.

"She certainly looks like she's feeling better," Jules said.

I couldn't take my eyes off of the couple. To be desired so strongly and so physically must be the most wonderful thing in the whole world. I wanted to be kissed like that.

"I don't know about you, but I'd say she's way ahead of me in this game she's forced us all to play. I haven't moved a step and she looks like she's quite comfortable out there in first place," Jules said.

I turned to Jules. Caught up in my own longing for physical touch, I leaned into the table and closed my eyes. My frustration was palatable and I was sure he could see my desire. My mouth was parched, but I felt too weak to lift the glass to my lips.

"It looks like she'll probably get the prize after all." Jules spoke, but I didn't hear his words. I imagined his tongue on my lips. I wanted to pull him close, to bring his face, the spray of freckles across his nose into me. I wanted to hold him like the woman across the way held her lover.

"Not that her win was ever in question," he said. "We weren't much competition for her."

I put my hand next to his. They were the same length. They would fit so perfectly together. One inside the other. His inside mine. The feel of his skin against mine.

I could scarcely breathe.

"Are you okay?" Jules asked. He touched my forehead with the back of his hand. I caught his wrist and held it as if I might faint without it.

"Everything all right, little one?"

"I'm fine," I whispered, then realizing I hadn't heard a word he had said. I asked who we were talking about.

"I just hope she knows him," Jules said.

"Who?" I asked.

"Sophie?" My sister's name ended my daydreams like a switch that had been dimmed.

When the woman stood, I realized at once what he had been talking about. "Oh my god," I said. "It's Sophie."

"Don't tell me you've just woken up to that fact," Jules said.

"I don't believe it."

She wore a black dress, one I had never seen on her before. It was pulled off her shoulders and fell just above her ankles. Around her neck was a tightly wrapped red and blue scarf. Her hair was piled on top of her head. She wore gold hoop earrings borrowed from my mother's jewelry box. She looked chic and much older than she usually did.

"I thought that's what had you so entranced."

The man stood and I recognized him too.

"That's Grandfather's doctor."

"Of course," Jules said. "That's who that is. From the airport."

They did not see us and we did nothing to draw attention our way. Arm in arm, they walked down the street. Sophie's skirt bounced back and forth, her heels clicking on the cobblestone.

When they were out of sight, Jules clapped. "Brava. She is a clever sort of girl, isn't she?"

I drank my coffee, licking the granules of sugar from the bottom of my cup. "Jules, do you think Sophie is capable of murder?"

He was surprised. "Are you worried about the doctor?"

"Not at all."

"It's not you, is it?" Jules asked. "Do you fear for your life?"

"I'm trying to determine the reason why we left Paris," I said. "Do you know? Did Sophie ever say anything to you?"

"We never talked about it," Jules said. "I just assumed you came down here because Paris is so rainy and gloomy. Dark and depressing."

Our Paris apartment felt far away, an unsolved mystery that no longer should be important and yet I felt if I only knew the answer, I would be able to control my future with more certainty.

"Are you sure there really was one?" Jules asked.

"Why wouldn't there have been?"

"I don't know," Jules said. "I guess because nothing in your family seems to be wrong."

"Maybe you're right," I said. Perhaps Father had simply used the idea of scandal as a ploy to get rid of us. He might have been unhappy. He might have thought it better to live alone, then with the burden of family—his father and two daughters.

But none of that was the least bit important anymore. Sophie had found someone, and I was on the Riviera with the man I intended to marry. It didn't matter anymore, but talking like this got Jules' attention and I used it as a method of flirtation.

"And yet what do I know?" Jules asked. "Families do have their secrets. Maybe Sophie murdered an important government official."

"That would certainly be a good reason to leave Paris," I said.

"Banished from France is more like it," Jules said.

"Well then, "I sighed. "That doesn't explain a thing."

*W*hen we got home, Mr. Tamarini was standing outside the gates of the Villa. Mr. Tamarini was the village handyman who came by the house to see if there was any work. Sophie had given him the job of trimming the vines, an impossible job, but he had worked for several days. His progress was slow and in the end, it looked no different than before he had started. Sophie dealt with him. I stayed away from him. He was an old man without many teeth in his mouth. He mumbled and confused me.

He approached the driver's side of the car and spoke to Jules.

Jules struggled to understand. "Who?"

Mr. Tamarini answered though what he said was cryptic and I let Jules ask the questions.

Several minutes later, Jules translated. "A Hilda Koch who lives down the road has invited your grandfather to tea."

"When?"

"I'm guessing now," Jules said. Mr. Tamarini had moved away from the car and was making his way down the mountainside. I knew we weren't going to get any clarification on that matter.

"Go get your Grandfather," Jules directed. "I'll drive him down to this woman's place."

"Are you sure you want to bother?" I asked. "Grandfather isn't a gracious person."

"Neither am I," Jules said. "But I can drive an old man to see his girlfriend."

"My grandfather is nearly blind. I don't think he has a girlfriend."

"Go," Jules waved me out of the car.

I ran to the house. Mathilde was in the garden cleaning the rugs. A thick rope was tied across two palm trees and she had thrown one rug over the rope. She beat on it with the end of a broom. The palm trees weren't strong or as sturdy as they might have been. They suffered under the weight of the rug. Mathilde looked up with the sound of my footfalls on the front steps. She stopped beating the rug and looked over to Jules who had his head back on the seat, eyes closed, sleeping in the strong afternoon sun.

I gave Grandfather the message. "You've been invited to tea at Hilda Koch's house."

"That woman must think I have money," Grandfather said. "This is the third time she's invited me to her house." He wore a pressed shirt and had combed his hair. I realized that this invitation was not a total surprise. His hair was wet at the ends and matted down; he had combed it for the occasion.

"Jules has offered to take you," I said.

"Jules?" Grandfather asked. "Who is Jules?"

"The short little man with the large motor car," I gave him his words as if they might jar his memory. "My friend. The one without a thought in his head and as far as you can tell, not much more in his wallet?"

Grandfather considered this as if he had several other options. "All right. That's acceptable. Fine. I'd be glad to let him take me there."

"I'll tell him," I said.

"Hilda is very fond of young people. Where's Sophie?"

The lie came easily. "She went to see the dentist."

"Are her teeth bothering her?"

"They must be," I said. "Why else would she spend so much time with someone of that sort?"

"Of what sort?" he asked. He was irritated. I did that to him. Without any effort—being around him was sufficient reason.

"The medical sort," I said.

"If she's not here, you better come along," Grandfather said. "That way if I stay late, I won't have to stumble home in the dark."

Grandfather was cordial to Jules. He started the conversation by commenting on the car—how it ran, how it did on the steep mountain roads, if gasoline was expensive. He asked about cleaning it, how the sea air damaged the exterior. Jules was also polite. I had hoped that Grandfather had reconsidered his initial impression of Jules. The chance that Jules might become family was always on my mind.

Hilda Koch's place was lower on the mountain than we were and instead of a courtyard, she had steep steps leading up to a balcony that wrapped around the turquoise house and looked as if it had been cobbled together over the years. And yet it was very pleasant. The gardens were filled with sun and light; there were no troublesome vines and her place had a wide-open view of the Mediterranean.

She was quite pleased to meet Jules and insisted he stay for tea.

Jules made an excuse of sorts. He didn't seem interested in staying.

"Everyone has time for tea," Hilda insisted. "Especially if it's mine." Hilda seemed amused by her own words and Jules had no choice but to accept her invitation, but he did so reluctantly and it seemed out of character.

Hilda was Dutch, a widow, who had spent most of her life in the South of France. "We came down here years ago," she said. "When these resorts were mere villages. We were the pioneers, the first ones. And then each year it became harder and harder to leave."

"What sense is leaving Paradise?" Jules asked.

"I like that," Hilda said. "I've often thought of this place as a kind of heaven on earth though judging by the crowds that now flock here every year, it's hardly an original thought."

Hilda hugged me and told me she remembered me as a little girl.

"You've become a beautiful young lady." She clapped her hands as if applauding me.

I hoped Jules was paying close attention.

A tea service was set on the table near the door. She asked if we wanted to see the house before or after our refreshments.

Touring people's houses wasn't something I was used to doing.

It wasn't done in France. I was intrigued that this woman took it for granted that we would want to see her house. Maybe it was a Dutch custom.

"I've seen the house," Grandfather said. "I don't guess it's changed in a week's time."

Hilda laughed. "Your grandfather is such an amusing man."

My guess was that Grandfather had made no attempt to be humorous.

Her house was worth touring. The large rooms all had grand views of the bay.

On the wall in the large foyer was a sketch—a pencil drawing of a woman on a chair, a balcony to her one side, a vase on the table beside her. Behind her were the open balcony doors and beyond it, the sea.

"It looks like Matisse," Jules said.

"Very good," Hilda said. "You know your local artists."

"I would hardly consider Matisse as a local artist," Jules said.

"But he does live here," Hilda said. "Which technically makes him local."

"He's one of the world's greatest artists. I don't think we need to classify him in a definition as small as local." Jules was being pedantic. I was used to it, but Hilda seemed at first taken aback by his strong opinion, then amused.

"He would be pleased to hear you say such things."

Jules stared at the sketch. "It's beautiful."

He put his face a few inches from the sketch. Hilda took it off the wall and gave it to him. "Go over to the window," she directed. "You'll be able to admire it more in the bright light."

"Does something like this cost a fortune?" Jules asked.

"It was a present."

"He gave it to you?" Jules said. "Matisse gave it to you?"

"He did," Hilda said. She wore a long skirt with a bird embroidered on the hip. Her hair was tucked into a neat bun at the nape of her neck. She was very graceful, very elegant.

"Do you know him?" Jules was taken by surprise by her casual attitude towards Matisse. I tried to turn the framed sketch so that I could see it, but Jules held too firm a grip. I worried that I would break it if I insisted he hand it over.

"He and my husband knew each other," Hilda said. "Occasionally we socialized with him."

Jules cradled the drawing, but Hilda held out her hands. She wanted to hang it back on the wall. Jules gave it up with much hesitation. He had a thousand questions for Hilda. He wanted to know everything about Matisse.

"You're a real admirer," Hilda said. "I'm impressed."

"I often go to Vence to try and catch a glimpse of him."

"Vence? I don't think he's living in Vence," Hilda said.

"At the *Villa La Reve*."

"That's his estate," Hilda said. "But I don't think he's there anymore." She paused. "What made me think he had moved?"

She searched but couldn't remember how she had known he was gone from Vence. I could tell from Jules' preoccupation with the sketch that he didn't think she knew anything anyway. After the tour, where Hilda showed us everything—even the bathrooms—we sat around the table for tea.

Hilda and Grandfather remembered for a while. It wasn't boring. Grandfather answered her questions in monosyllables, so it was mostly Hilda telling stories of the past. She was a good talker. She stayed on subject and her stories were not just random memories—they came to satisfying conclusions.

"The Côte d'Azur has always been enticing," Hilda explained. "I'm an old woman who may be glorifying the past, but I did think that the years before the war were somehow more magical. Perhaps less gaudy. The beaches were always empty, not the crowds you see nowadays."

"What good is an empty beach?" Jules asked.

Hilda laughed. "We found plenty to do on those empty beaches, didn't we, Sebastian?"

I smiled. Grandfather's name was Sebastian, but no one ever called him that.

"My mind doesn't go back that far," Grandfather said.

Hilda nodded. "We did. We all did. It was wonderful. There were elegant women carrying flowered parasols. Men wore white linen suits. They sauntered the boardwalks with nothing to do but sit at a café and sip Pernod." She laughed, happy with her memories. "We used to spend time on 'le grand jetée,' the old steel pier in Nice. It was destroyed in the war, but at one time it was the meeting place for everyone chic on the Riviera. Old Moorish theaters, casinos. Believe me when I say it was quite an exciting place to be."

"I don't think it's changed all that much," I said. "It's still a wonderful place." I turned to Jules. "Wouldn't you agree, Jules?"

Jules was bored. He finished his tea in two large swallows, ate a cake in just as many bites.

Hilda Koch was an astute woman; she sensed that she did not have a captive audience.

"Enough of yesterday," Hilda announced and refilled our teacups.

"Would you mind if I went back in and looked at the Matisse sketch?" Jules stood.

He was being deliberately rude. She was obviously enjoying her tea party but if she was irritated or bothered by his behavior, she did not show it. "By all means. I'm glad you admire it. Please, act in my house as you would act in yours."

Jules, hands in pocket, slouched into the house.

Hilda continued playing host. She talked of the summer winds, of the upcoming festivals along the coast, and the possibility that the Prince of Monaco would marry soon. She paused and I smiled at her. "I've been meaning to ask someone," she said. "Do you have trouble with theft on your side of the mountain?

"Theft?" I asked.

Grandfather got up to smoke a cigarette near the railings. Jules came out a few minutes later and joined him. Grandfather had his own cigarettes but asked Jules for one.

"You know, people coming in and taking things."

"I don't think so," I said. "At least not while we've been living here."

"I find it most curious," Hilda said. "They must have come in when we were at the market the other day."

"What did they take?" I asked.

"My figurines," Hilda said. "I'm a collector of figurines. I've spent years searching them out. Little animals. Exotic elephants. Colorful birds. I know it sounds like a child's game, but they're actually quite valuable. Most of them are hand painted. The detail work is quite delicate. I had more than twenty-five from as many countries."

"Perhaps you've only misplaced them?" I asked.

"They're not easy to misplace," Hilda said.

"Did you move them one day?"

"I am an old woman, but I am not forgetful." She sat up very straight in her chair and sipped her tea. Her fingers wrapped around the gold-painted handle of the cup and I was sorry that she had lost the things she treasured.

"You remember, Sebastian," Hilda talked to Grandfather. "You saw them. I had them lined up on the table near the big window there." She nodded towards the house. "I showed them to you the other night. My little creatures from around the world."

Grandfather shook his head.

"They were right here. On the table near the big window. You must remember them, Sebastian?" Hilda asked. "My little china creatures from around the world?"

"I am an old man, but unlike you, I am unfortunately forgetful," Grandfather said.

"You must remember the figurines," Hilda said. "I showed them to you. They were precious little things. So colorful. So wonderful. I've been collecting them for years."

"What about the maid?" I asked. "Perhaps she moved them when she was cleaning."

"I don't have a maid," Hilda said.

"No?" I asked. I thought to tell her that she could have ours. Mathilde might be thrilled to work for Hilda Koch. Mathilde would probably have been thrilled to work for anyone but us.

Jules came back and ended Hilda's talk about her lost figurines when he said it was time that he got going. "I'd be happy to give you a lift home, sir," he addressed Grandfather.

I thought Grandfather would want to stay, but Hilda stood and told him he shouldn't give up the chance to ride in such an impressive automobile.

"My granddaughters are spoiled," Grandfather said. "They ride in the Cadillac like it's their own private bus."

"Well that's what love does," Hilda said. "It transforms the world."

Jules had walked ahead and I didn't know if he heard Hilda's remark. I beamed. I wanted to think that we had given her the impression that we were in love, though I wasn't sure this was possible given Jules' uncharacteristically surly behavior.

On the way down to the car, I asked Jules if he was feeling all right. "You seem upset," I said, deliberately avoiding the word "rude."

"Old people are always the same."

"She was kind," I said.

"But mostly dull," Jules said. "And batty," Jules said. "She knew Matisse. Matisse, the greatest artist in the world, and what does she choose to talk about? The beach. An old pier that hasn't been there in nearly a decade?"

"You like the beach," I reminded him.

"Not even today's beach. But what it used to look like." He waved his hands to the bay. "I don't know about you, but my guess is that not much has changed with the physical world."

"She talked of other things."

"She called Matisse a local artist," Jules pressed his palms together. "Diminishing his talents to call him local. "

There was no sense arguing. He had made his mind up; he ranted all the way to the car.

"If I was going to take anything from that house, it wouldn't be some silly figurines," Jules said, as we were getting into the car. "I'd take the Matisse. That's the only thing worth stealing."

Hilda stood at the railings. I looked up and waved goodbye. She was too far away to hear Jules' disrespectful words.

I found Sophie in the bathtub. She had a book and a cigarette; the ashtray was precariously balanced on the rounded edge. The soaked cigarette and mash of tobacco told me that she had already knocked it into the water once before.

The bath was full, but she continued to let the taps run. I leaned over and turned them off. "It ruins the ceiling when you overflow the water onto the floor."

"I'm like a boat," she said. "A gigantic boat in a small ocean." She was not drunk, but giddy. This must have been what kissing did to a person's mind. It made them regress.

"We took Grandfather to visit Hilda Koch," I said.

"Isn't that funny that they've met up again?" Sophie asked. "After all these years? She was such a beautiful woman when she was younger. They used to have the most exotic parties. I remember they had bowls of olives on every table. They had musicians. Men playing instruments. People dressed up. It was always lovely."

"You should go down and reminisce with her," I said. "She likes to talk about the past."

"And Grandfather likes that?"

"He seemed happy enough."

"Do you think there's anything romantic between the two of them?"

I couldn't imagine an attraction between Grandfather and Hilda. Grandfather was so dull and so pessimistic. Hilda was old, but she was still amused by life. "She's so much more interesting than Grandfather. She talks about art and restaurants. She knows her history. Grandfather would bore her to an early grave."

Sophie sank into the water. Her legs were too long and she had to balance her toes on the opposite edge.

"And what about you?" I asked.

"Me what?"

"Did you have a good day?"

"Yes, thank you. I did." Sophie took the washcloth and squeezed out the excess water onto her knees. The room was warm but when I suggested opening the window, Sophie said the night air would cool the water too quickly.

"Did you stay here?" I said.

"I didn't," she said. "I did a few boring errands."

"They couldn't have been that boring," I said.

"And why is that?"

I stood up and went to the mirror. I pulled my hair on top of my head, a style I did not wear—it was too sophisticated for me—but the way Sophie had worn her hair that day. "Because you don't seem bored."

"I'm not now," she said. "No one's ever bored when they're taking a bath."

"I'd rather go to a café."

"You can't get clean in a café."

Sophie thought she was fooling me and I let her believe that for awhile.

I waited while she readied for bed. When I heard the click of the lamp at her bedside table, I walked down the hall and stood in her darkened doorway.

"What's his name?" I asked.

She was not asleep. She sat up and asked me what I wanted.

"Grandfather's doctor," I said. "I was just curious about his first name."

"What's this?"

"Does he have one?" I asked.

"I'm sure he does," she said.

"And what is it?"

"Perhaps you should ask Grandfather, though I'd wait until morning. It's late. I'm sure he's asleep by now."

"Grandfather's forgetful," I said.

"He is," she said. "But he likes his doctor."

"Not as much as you do," I said.

She flicked on the bedside light. The room filled with shadows and our bodies looked huge as they moved up the walls to the ceilings.

"What are you doing, Agnes?" She still acted naïve.

"I saw you," I said. "This afternoon. In Monte Carlo. At the café."

She covered her face. Not in shame, but in pleasure. She wasn't humiliated, but happy. She took her hands from her face and bit the side of her hand as if afraid that she might yell out in happiness.

She motioned me into the room. "Be quiet."

I went in and closed the door. She was sitting up in bed, rocking herself with a wide grin on her face. "You didn't tell Grandfather, did you?"

"Sophie," I sighed.

"I'm in love," she said and opened her arms dramatically. Her nightgown had tiny blue and white laces on the bodice, which she had not tied. Her skin was dark like mine. We had both spent many hours in the sun.

"Congratulations," I said.

"That's a strange thing to tell someone when they've just told you that they are in love," she said.

"It was your idea."

"My what?"

"Because of the competition," I said. "Jules is already calling you the winner."

"Jules saw us, too?"

"You weren't exactly discreet. Half the residents on the Riviera saw you," I said.

She grabbed me and pulled me down into the bed, giggling and carrying on like she had lost control of her senses. The bedsheets smelled of lavender and laundry soap and I giggled with her.

She hugged and kissed my hair. She squealed and I called her a pig.

"Is it great?" I asked.

She knew exactly what I was talking about. "Being in love is better than great," she said.

"That's what it looked like," I said, thinking back to when I saw her arms wrapped around his neck.

She squealed again. She really was a pig. "He's wonderful. Richard is the most wonderful man I've ever met. It's like a dream."

Grandfather was up. His hearing was suddenly sensitive and he complained of not being able to sleep well at night because of all the noises of the house. "I hear the animals running about. People whispering. Everyone moving about." He blamed it on his failing eyesight, but I think he was bored. He slept most afternoons and woke at night because he had had too much sleep. He shuffled to the steps and called up. "What's going on up there?"

"Nothing, Grandfather," I went to the door and called down. "It's just us," I reassured him.

It was quiet. I heard the study door shut.

I went back to the bed. Sophie had straightened the covers.

"He's almost perfect."

I heard what she said, but didn't think it meant anything other than Sophie admitting that Richard had faults, which was hardly a surprise. People had faults. I thought it was a woman in love admitting that her man might not be a fantasy.

I fell asleep immediately but woke in the middle of the night, hours before dawn. The room was stuffy and closed in. I got up and went to the windows. I pushed open the shutters and sat on the sill looking out into the darkness. The air smelled of warm pines. The moon, a tiny sliver, was on its back, too lazy to stand upright; it was dozing until dawn.

I thought about love and how I did not really understand it. I worried. People in love acted like my sister Sophie and the doctor. They did not act like chums, which is what I felt Jules thought of me. I needed to bridge that gap. The days were passing. I would have to do more.

A nighthawk swooped low in the sky, hovering over the garden shed. Its radar caught sight of the open window and it came over to inspect. I feared it would fly in the window. It came close but then a cloud passed in front of moon, the night air lost its glow and the hawk flew off. I went back to bed.

Chapter Six

Sophie was already dressed and ready to leave the house when I came down the next morning. She drank her bowl of coffee and milk in several quick gulps and I knew she had no time for me right then.

"It's lovely, isn't it?" she asked.

"The coffee?" I asked.

"The Riviera," she said and did a little box step dance. "We should have moved here years ago."

The bread truck horn blew and she told me to enjoy the beautiful day. "I plan to enjoy mine," she said. I followed her into the kitchen where she tossed her dishes into the sink, then asked me to take care of them for her. "Don't leave them or Cook will have my head," she directed, wiping croissant crumbs from her face and lips.

"Where are you off to?" I asked.

"I can't miss the ride," she said. She winked, then disappeared out the back door.

I watched as she ran across the garden. It was wild, the weeds and flowers growing together. Behind the villa was a narrow, unpaved lane. The bread truck, the dairyman, and the vegetable carts used it as a way to get goods to the hamlet of houses surrounding ours.

Cook was there, talking with the other women who were waiting for their daily supplies of bread and croissants.

Sophie greeted the driver—this was obviously not the first time she had taken a ride with him—then climbed into the passenger side of the truck. She sat sideways with her long legs tucked into the tiny space. She took out a small mirror and combed her hair using her compact to guide her.

The truck moved on and a few minutes later, Cook brought in the bread.

"Everyone is up and about this morning," she said. "Quite an early crew. Where's your Grandfather?"

"I haven't seen him," I said. When Grandfather had trouble sleeping at night, he sometimes slept all morning, aggravating the problem further.

I watched the blue truck as it moved down the narrow lane and disappeared from my sight.

Cook whistled, a thin sound through her teeth. "I'd bet money this whole thing involves a man," Cook said, as she set the fresh goods onto the counter.

She stopped me before I could respond. "Don't tell me because I don't want to be in the middle of anything. If your Grandfather questions me about Sophie's whereabouts, I can say I have no idea. I can tell him I saw her leave with the bread man, but that's all I know."

But of course it wasn't. She and the other women had spent the last fifteen minutes gossiping about Sophie. The bread man was probably also a great source of gossip and they had, more than likely, bribed him to tell where he dropped Sophie every morning.

I admired Sophie's way of getting what she wanted. The bus was reliable, but slow. And the bread man went straight to Menton after he made his runs up on the mountainside. It was clever of her to think of another mode of transportation.

I broke off a piece of croissant and nibbled it. Its freshness was one of my favorite tastes.

Cook scolded me. "Use a plate," she said.

I got one down, but that wasn't good enough for Cook, who liked to tell people what to do.

"The coffee pot is in the dining room," Cook said. "I'm not going to serve breakfast in every room in this house."

I ate alone, quickly. Grandfather was up now and his radio was loud with the morning news. He listened to everything. First the national news, then the local broadcasts, which included the farm reports, the weather reports. When it started again the next hour, he'd listen all over, rapt as if hearing it for the first time.

Mathilde came in to clear breakfast dishes. There weren't many. Just mine. Grandfather had his coffee in his study. Mathilde took the dishes and carried the tray to the door, then came back in the room. She set the tray back on the table. She looked at me strangely, as if she was going to scold me.

"What?" I asked.

"Your friend," she said. "The one with the big black car."

"What about him?"

"What's his name?" she spoke slowly.

"Jules," I answered.

She laughed and clapped her hands together, terribly pleased about something.

"Do you think that's a funny name?" I asked.

"I don't know. Do you?" she said, and picked up the tray.

"Not at all, but I'm not the one with the big smile."

She shifted the balance of the tray onto her hip. I heard the rattle of cups and saucers, but they did not hit the floor.

She does drink, I thought, and vowed to remember to tell Sophie to start locking up the liquor. At the very least, Sophie should hide the bottles.

*J*ules was later than usual. He was in a terrible temper. "We have been deceived," he said the minute he saw me.

"We have?" I asked. I shut the door and turned towards him.

"Most definitely," Jules said. He adjusted his cap and started the engine.

"By whom?"

"By everyone," Jules said. There was not much room between the stone posts at the gate, but Jules did not hesitate. He drove straight through, the gravel spewing out behind us.

"They've lied to us. Out-and-out lied to us."

"They have?" I asked.

"They have," Jules said.

"Why?"

"I don't know," Jules said. "I guess it amused them to think us fools."

"How are we fools?" I asked.

"Because we didn't know about Matisse," Jules said.

Except for the bread lady in Vence who thought we were writing a book on Matisse's early life (I assumed this was what Jules must have told her), I couldn't think of anyone we had talked to about Matisse. Even Sophie was in the dark when it came to Jules' passions.

"I don't understand," I said.

"He's gone," Jules announced. He slammed his fists on the steering wheel and the car for several seconds lost its grip on the road.

"Matisse is dead?" I yelped.

"Of course he's not dead," Jules said. We had stopped at the first intersection, an almost blind left turn. Jules inched out. It was always a bit thrilling to see if another car wasn't speeding along the main road. We had had plenty of near misses. "He's just gone."

"Gone where?" I imagined him in Paris, being feted by the cognoscenti of the art world.

"He hasn't been in Vence for months," Jules was speaking at an incredible speed. He drove just as fast. The pace and the curves made my stomach turn in a most exciting way.

"What about the villa?" I asked.

"It seems that everybody knew this to be true. He hasn't lived in Vence in almost a year. That old Dutch woman was right."

"Hilda?" I asked.

"She knew he was gone," Jules said. "She told me I was wrong the other day when we were there. I should have listened. It would have saved some time."

"That was two days ago."

"Two days is two days," Jules said. "I don't like being the fool.

Think of all those wasted trips. Days spent driving to that godforsaken little village."

"I thought you liked it."

"I liked it when I knew Matisse was living there," Jules said. "Without Matisse, it's just a little village with nothing to offer anyone but a plaque that says 'a great artist once painted here'."

"There's the Chappelle du Rosaire," I said.

"Unfinished." Jules brushed away this structure as if it was nothing. "It won't be his masterpiece unless it's completed, which it doesn't look like it will be. Not in his lifetime."

We had driven by the hotel many times—it was one of the many places we had toured when Jules was giving me a retrospective of Matisse's life.

"He's been here all along," Jules said. "Right in Nice."

The hotel was in the foothills above Nice, a large Edwardian structure that looked like a gigantic birthday present waiting for a giant to scoop it up and take it away: The Hotel Regina.

We parked the car a few blocks from the Hotel—the roads up in Cimiez neighborhood were narrow and Jules had a hard time maneuvering the Cadillac. We marched towards the Hotel, two soldiers ready to do battle, when suddenly Jules took my arm and veered me towards a side street running to the right of the main boulevard.

"What?" I asked. I could see the Hotel. So could he. I didn't understand the sudden change of direction.

"I know a shortcut," Jules said. He walked ahead, pulling my elbow so that I would follow.

The street was clearly marked as a dead end. "I don't think this will work," I said.

"It's worth a try."

I didn't understand his sudden desire for speed. We had waited this long to catch a glimpse of Matisse, what did a few minutes matter?

The street was lined with shops—the bakery, the butcher, and the vegetable stands. We found a space for the car near some garbage bins. We got out and walked back in the direction of the hotel.

A man came towards us. He said Jules' name several times but Jules was uncharacteristically interested in the chickens hanging in the butcher's window.

"That man is speaking to you," I said.

"Jules Agard. Jules Agard."

It was impossible to miss, loud and clear, but Jules was oblivious. "Is he?"

"Open your ears," I said and turned to watch the man coming towards us. "He's calling your name."

"Maybe you misheard."

"I don't think so," I said.

When the man was two feet away and practically shouting Jules' name, Jules turned, acting as if the man's presence had taken him completely by surprise. "Oh, hello there. How are you?" He shook the man's hand, polite but without his usual smile.

The man was out of breath. He stopped and coughed into his white handkerchief, then shoved it back into his pocket.

"It's a beautiful day, isn't it?" Jules asked.

But the man was not interested in discussing the weather. He addressed Jules sternly. "You are a man, I assume, who takes care of his bills."

"Without a doubt," Jules said.

The man waited for Jules to finish his sentence. I, too, thought he was going to say more. Other shoppers pushed their way around us; we were a small island of non-movement. I was curious and stayed as close to Jules as I could.

"Without a doubt I am a man who takes care of his bills."

"Well then," the man said.

"Yes?" Jules inquired.

"Well then, without a doubt I can expect a payment."

"Without a doubt," Jules said.

But the man was no longer amused by their little word game.

"Today," the man said.

"Of course," Jules said. "Today."

"Good," the man said.

"Without a doubt," Jules said, with much less conviction than the first time.

"Then good day to you and the young woman," the man lifted his hat a few inches from his head and turned around to walk back to the main boulevard.

The butcher was still waiting to make the sale. "Shall I wrap one up for you, sir?" he asked Jules, but looked to me. I shrugged. I had no use for a chicken.

Jules shook his head. "No. I don't think that would be a good idea. Not today of all days."

*W*e walked back to the car. I didn't need to ask about the Hotel Regina. I knew without asking that our plans had changed.

"I'm afraid Matisse is going to have to wait," Jules said.

"He's waited this long," I said. "A few more hours shouldn't matter."

"Would you mind if we left Nice?" Jules asked.

"Of course not," I said. "We'll have fun wherever we go. Without a doubt."

My joke got no response from Jules. I stated the obvious. "You owe that man money?"

"I need to see to something," Jules said. He was distracted, but then seemed to make a decision. We drove to Monte Carlo and parked the car outside the large casino. Sophie and I had been in one of the smaller casinos in Menton. The doorman had joked about the danger of allowing two unaccompanied women into the casino. "Maybe you should come with us," Sophie had flirted back. "We don't have the slightest idea of what we're supposed to do in here."

"You are supposed to win money," the doorman had told her.

"What if we don't have much to start with?"

"I'd advise the slot machines," the doorman said. "Besides, you're not dressed appropriately for the other rooms."

I thought the casino shabby and dark and after a few tries at the slot machine and coming up with nothing asked Sophie if we could go. As we had no money and no one offered us a drink, we left. Sophie thought it exciting. I thought there was something sinister about the whole thing.

The casino in Monte Carlo was much larger than the one in Menton, but it shared many of the same qualities—mostly that it was a place that had once been nice, but the elegance was long gone.

The rooms were large, dark; the chandeliers that hung from the ceilings were too high as if they had been pulled up to be cleaned and then forgotten. The room smelled and I put my hand over my mouth.

"What is that?" I asked.

"Awful, isn't it?" Jules said. He put his mouth to my ear and whispered the reason for the foul odor.

The old women who lined the black jack tables wore sponges between their legs so they would not have to waste time going to the bathroom. The large rooms with the fans and open windows stank of urine, which the woman blamed on their dogs, scolding them for not holding their pee. "Be a good girl and wait for Mommy to take you outside. Be a good girl."

The croupiers wore tuxedo jackets and black bow ties. They were tall, hovering above everyone. They taped their pull sticks on the side of the tables.

Jules took me to the slot machine room.

"Wait here," he said. But I was afraid to be without him. There was something creepy about the scene going on in front of us. The string of women lined up along the wall in front of their machines were menacing, and at any moment I thought their intensity would redirect to me.

"Wait," I called after him.

"Stay," he said. "Don't worry. I'll be right back."

He left and I counted to ten.

He was still not back. I counted to ten again. Then I felt so uncomfortable I followed him into the room.

It had a different feel than the slot machine room. The carpet had once been patterned, but the different colors of the carpet had faded so that the flowers and vines were suggested now. Cigarette smoke hung like fog.

Jules was talking to an older woman. Her back was to me, but she turned and looked at me. She had a net in her hair and wore a black dress and thick black tights. She had a large chest covered with her cigarette ashes. Jules took the cigarette from her and put it out in the freestanding ashtray next to the machine. She pulled the arm and I watched the viewer. A flicker of color stopped for a moment; then she pulled the arm again.

He called her *Cherie* and they talked for some time. Then he said it was time he left. I had grown used to the smell and shabbiness of the place by then.

I hoped there were other, grander, rooms. I thought the cocktail lounges would be more sophisticated. I imagined them to be glamorous with large patios and private balconies with views of the Mediterranean. I didn't see any sign to support the existence of these imaginary rooms.

"Agnes," Jules said. "I told you to wait for me in the other room."

"I waited," I said. "Then I thought you had gone."

I was not sure why he was so angry, but he was upset that I had deliberately disobeyed.

Jules nodded his head. Whatever business he had there, he was done. He took my arm and led me to the entranceway.

The doorman held the door open for us.

"Who was that?" I asked as we stepped outside.

"I didn't want you in that room," he said. He was being boring and I told him so.

"You have to listen to me," he said.

"Did you borrow money from her? Are you going to pay back that man?"

Jules didn't answer right away and I, thinking he hadn't heard, asked again. "Is she a professional gambler?"

"I'm sure you're familiar with the expression, 'curiosity killed the cat'?" Jules asked.

"I know the expression quite well, but it doesn't answer any of my questions," I said firmly.

The street traffic was loud; horns and engines. The small turnabout outside the casino was lined with cars and the traffic was loud. Horns and motor engines prevented me from hearing exactly what he said.

"Tell me," I insisted. "Who was that foul woman?"

Jules stopped and spoke quietly. "What if I told you that woman was my mother?"

I laughed. I didn't really get the joke but I knew there had to be one.

"Is that funny?" he asked.

"How can that be your mother?" I said, and waited for the punch line.

"It can't be?" he asked.

"Of course not," I said emphatically. "How could it be?"

"That's right," Jules said, and suddenly he grinned. "How could it be?"

I was relieved that we were laughing. "Your mother lives in Marseilles. With your Father, right? Is he still a lawyer? Is he still practicing law?"

Jules stopped to retie his espadrilles and I waited for him before crossing the street.

"Is he still working?"

"No," Jules said, when he stood. "He isn't."

"He's retired?" I asked.

Jules nodded. "Yes. That's right."

"I'm sure he's still admired," I said.

"No," Jules said. "He's not."

"Why? What happened?"

"He's dead, Agnes."

I hadn't realized Jules' father was dead and was just about to ask about him, when Jules held up his hand. But I was belligerent and insisted.

"Let's not talk about it anymore. It's boring. The whole subject is tiring."

"Just tell me who the woman is and I'll shut up about everything else."

"She is someone I know," Jules said. "How about we leave it at that?"

"Is it what the landscape demands?" I asked and when Jules grinned and took my hand, the doubts and confusion I had felt a moment ago disappeared.

"What the landscape demands" was Jules' expression. He had passion for certain things, but I noticed he dismissed any talk of things of great importance. I had once confided in him about my mother's death—something that usually earned most people's sympathy—but Jules reacted differently.

"Death is terrible," he said.

"It is," I nodded. "I think everyone would agree with you."

But he meant that it was a terrible thing to talk about. "Let's change the subject. Quickly. Death doesn't go with the scenery down here. It jars. The landscape demands that we talk of happy things."

I felt stupid. I hadn't meant to depress him. But I had been looking for ways to increase my intimacy with Jules and I thought that I might use my mother's death as a means to impress him. I wanted to show him that, though I was only fifteen, I had suffered. Instead his rebuff of my personal tragedy struck me as cold and I wondered how to get closer to someone who so obviously didn't want to talk on that level. A lover was supposed to be someone you told your secrets to, someone you shared your fears with. But Jules wasn't the type to want to know secrets or fears. How did a woman get a man to talk on a more intimate level? It was something I would have to discuss with Sophie, though of course, I wouldn't mention any names.

Chapter Seven

*D*espite all the predictions that the Chapelle du Rosaire in Vence would never be finished, Matisse completed the work in early June.

"They say it's glorious," Jules reported.

We had made a few attempts to see Matisse at the Hotel Regina, but the hotel staff was discrete and tight-lipped about their residents. They wanted to know who we were with all our questions and they never validated our belief that Matisse was back living in an apartment there.

"We have to see it," Jules determined.

"Are we allowed?" I asked.

"Why wouldn't we be?"

"Is it open to the public?" I asked.

"I hardly think of us as the public."

The Bishop of Nice and the Dominican Sisters of Vence were planning the consecration, after which the chapel would be officially open. Jules had been told that it was a very private affair, an invitation-only celebration of Matisse's work.

"How can we get an invitation?" I asked.

"That's a good question."

The search for an invitation to the ceremony became our new quest.

We went to the chapel in Vence. It was on a small side street set into the mountainside. The tall gold and black spire rising up to the sky was the only clue that it was anything but a typical white painted house. The palm trees bracketing the chapel cast elongated shadows on the bright white walls.

There were several women working on the property. They moved slowly in the warm summer afternoon. Their brooms lazily smacked against the bricks lining the garden walls.

Jules and I went up to the gate. Jules was silent for several moments. I sensed he was thinking of how to explain our plight, then he walked boldly up to the woman who was sweeping the steps.

"Excuse me," he said. "I'm hoping you can help us."

She stopped sweeping and came over to talk to us.

"Do you know anything about the consecration ceremony?" Jules asked politely.

"I know that it is to take place in two weeks time," she said.

"We are devotees of Matisse," he explained. "And feel it is only right that we be included in this very special night."

"The chapel will be open to the public after the first of July," the woman explained. "I'm sure you'll get a chance to see it then."

"Some people consider him only a local artist, but my young friend and I understand and appreciate the enormity of his international reputation."

"A few friends and select members of the community have been sent invitations," the woman said. "Everyone else will have to wait."

"We would like to see it as soon as possible."

"All in good time," the woman said.

"Will Matisse be at the opening?"

"Would Molière have missed seeing one of his plays performed?"

"I haven't the slightest idea how to answer that question," Jules said. "You are aware that he's been having difficulties. Physically, that is."

For a minute I thought he was talking of Moliere, who I had always thought was dead.

"He is expected," she reported, then excused herself. "There's so much work to be done."

Jules turned away, deep in thought. "It's my one opportunity to meet him."

"I don't think we'll get an invitation."

"He'll be there. I know he will," Jules said. We walked towards the center of Vence. "I could talk to him. I know everything about his art. I'll just tell him the truth. That I've idolized his work and devotion to art for as long as I can remember."

"And that you think he's a deity."

"I'll probably leave that part out," Jules said.

He spent the next few days searching for ways to get an invitation to the opening night. He went to the mayor's office in Nice and asked if there was something he could fill out to get his name on the list. The man at the desk looked confused and after several questions advised us to come back. We did and someone new was working. We had to explain the whole situation to him. He said he hadn't any idea how to help us.

I told Jules not to worry. There was still time. "We'll find a way."

"There's not that much time," Jules said.

*I*n the end, it was Hilda Koch who gave Jules and me the opportunity to go to the ceremony. She had tickets to the consecration, but was not comfortable driving the coastal mountain roads in the evening light. Grandfather said she was quite disappointed not to be able to go.

I offered Jules as a chauffeur for the night.

Hilda thought it was a splendid idea.

When I gave Jules the news, he closed his eyes and held my hands as if I was a priest and he was asking for my blessing. "Tell me you're not joking, Agnes."

"I'm not joking," I said.

"I have an invitation?"

"Yes," I said. "You'll come with us."

Jules called me a genius and he kissed my hands several times. "This is joy," he said. "Real joy."

I loved his happiness and was thrilled that I was the one responsible for his elation. I wanted to stretch out the moment forever. He was grateful for me. Grateful for what I had brought him.

Sophie heard about our soiree and asked if she might come along.

"Maybe Grandfather's doctor is interested in chapels."

"Strangely enough, I think he's very fond of Matisse," Sophie said. "Maybe I will ask him if he'd like to come with us."

"Grandfather would probably like to have his doctor along," I said. "He'll be in heaven."

"I've never considered that angle," Sophie smiled.

Sophie and I spent the entire afternoon getting ready for the big night. I borrowed her slim black skirt and tried on several of her scarves.

"Can I wear any of them?" I asked.

"If that makes you happy," Sophie said. She was nervous because she had not found a way to tell Grandfather that Richard was joining us.

I ironed my clothes and, because she was being so generous, I ironed hers as well. Sophie washed and tied up my hair. She used hairspray and so many pins I thought I would faint under the weight. She sprayed lavender water on my neck and wrists and let me use her make-up, but then told me to wash off the lipstick. "It's too dark," she said. "It doesn't suit you."

Hilda had invited everyone for cocktails. Grandfather greeted Richard with some confusion. But Richard laughed it away. He had an easy charm and a huge laugh. He didn't exactly explain why he was there and said how much he was looking forward to the evening.

"I told you he was coming," Sophie said.

I liked her approach. A lie. Grandfather didn't like to be reminded that he forgot things; he simply accepted that it was a part of the evening's plan.

"You're not worried about my health, are you?" Grandfather asked.

"Not in the least," Richard answered.

"Maybe you should be," Grandfather said.

Grandfather got in Richard's car and told us again to hurry. "Hilda's very cross when people are late. The Dutch are punctual."

"He doesn't know any Dutch besides her," Sophie said. "And seeing that she'd lived her life on the Riviera, she's more French than Dutch. The French are always late."

"Not as late as the Italians," Jules said.

"Is that right, darling?" Sophie asked.

"But the worst are the Portuguese," he informed us.

"Really? Who would have guessed that?"

Richard and Grandfather drove away. Sophie wasn't happy about that arrangement, but it would have been awkward to say something.

"Not to worry," Jules said. "I'll make sure you get to go with the good doctor when we leave the old lady's house."

"Hilda," I told him.

Jules told Sophie and me we looked ravishing. Sophie turned around and modeled her outfit. It was a light blue, with a full skirt and a tight white bodice. She wore no jewelry. She looked airy and free and very happy. She told me to turn around so Jules could admire me. But I said no. "Jules isn't interested in seeing me," I said, trying to tease out the response I wanted.

Luckily Jules protested. "Of course I am."

Sophie held my hand as I modeled my skirt for him. Sophie's skirt was a bit long and I thought I might look like a child playing with her mother's clothes, but I stood as tall as I could. My hair felt like a crown and I kept opening my compact to check out the sleek line of my jaw. I thought I looked sophisticated.

Jules called us princesses.

"Then you must be our prince, *darling*," Sophie said.

She held the door open for me so I could climb in the back. I said something about her not being the only one unhappy with the driving arrangements.

She used her tight skirt as an excuse. "How could I possibly climb all the way back there, sweet one?"

I got in. It was not a night to argue or to be petty.

Sophie told Jules to drive slowly. "We don't want the wind messing our hair."

He drove recklessly and a minute later we were behind Richard and Grandfather.

Sophie introduced Richard as Grandfather's doctor, which amused Hilda.

"Is taking care of Sebastian one of the more important roles in your life?" she asked.

"The most important service," Richard said. His eyes were blue, the exact color of the Mediterranean. He smiled and flirted with Hilda.

"That's quite a life," Hilda flirted back.

We drank Kir Royales—champagne and crème de casiss— lovely pink drinks in wine glasses. There were tiny plates of appetizers on a large tray. Grandfather sat down and started eating as if he hadn't had a meal in days.

The rest of us stood at the balcony and admired the view.

Richard was exactly as Sophie had described him—he was perfect. His hair was black, his eyes bright blue. He had a dimple in the middle of his chin that was more pronounced when he smiled, which he did almost non-stop. He was incredibly happy with the evening. He complimented Hilda on her beautiful house, on her view, on her lovely dress. He told me I looked lovely, that he had never met a young lady of such charm and grace. He told Grandfather he seemed to be in tip-top shape. He said all this, but it was obvious that he couldn't keep his eyes off Sophie.

He was smitten. They touched, they laughed, and they stared

at each other. They brushed hips. I watched their secret dance and was envious.

I don't think Hilda was fooled that his accompanying us to the opening of the Chapel in Vence was medicinal.

I thought Jules could take some lessons from Richard. But all Jules was interested in was everyone being aware about the chapel's history. "Matisse had been working on the design without interruption since 1947. It's his present to the village of Vence where he sought refuge during the war. Matisse was advised to leave France. There was a huge fear that the Germans were going to bomb Nice and France didn't want to lose its most valued treasure, but he wouldn't go. He said, 'if everyone who has any value leaves France, what remains of France?' He moved instead to Vence."

Hilda complimented him on his knowledge.

Jules told us more stories of Matisse. He took Richard in and showed him the sketch.

The white sails of the boats shimmered in the bay below us. It was festive and I drank my champagne quickly and accepted Hilda's offer of more.

"This is like the old times, isn't it, Sebastian?" Hilda asked.

"We were young," Grandfather said.

"Is that what it is?" Hilda sighed. "I look at their youth and am reminded of my own age."

"Exactly."

"That's a dour attitude."

"But the truth."

"I don't believe it."

She went inside and put on an enormous hat that covered her entire face. Jules stood when she came out and told her she had to ride in his car. "I wouldn't want anything to happen to that hat," he said.

"It's magnificent, isn't it?" Hilda asked.

"I'll say," Jules agreed. He helped Grandfather and Hilda into the Cadillac and I motioned for Sophie to go with Richard.

She was demure. "If you think that's for the best."

"I do," I said.

*T*he entire village of Vence turned out for the opening. They stood on the streets. Only a select few were invited inside the gates. We waited for Sophie and Richard until Jules grew too impatient and suggested we go in.

"Do you think perhaps they're lost?" Grandfather asked.

"They were right behind us," Jules said. "I wouldn't worry."

"They might have taken a wrong road," I said. "It's confusing, isn't it, Jules?"

Jules agreed. "They'll get here eventually."

But I was right in thinking that they would not show up.

We went in. The man announced our arrival: Hilda Koch and friends.

The outside of the chapel looked like all the other structures on the hillside—white stucco made brighter and almost impossible to look at when the sun was high.

A trio of men gave welcome speeches. I was still feeling the effects of Hilda's champagne and didn't listen. Instead I thought about what it would be like to have Richard as my brother-in-law. It would be pleasant. They would have blue-eyed happy children who I could take care of. I could teach them to play in the surf, to pay attention to the waves, but not to be afraid of the ocean.

Jules was agitated. "I don't see him."

"Do you know what he looks like?"

"I'll know when I see him."

I asked Hilda if she had seen anything of Matisse, but she laughed. "My hat is so large it's difficult to see anyone."

The Bishop of Nice stood on the steps near the entranceway and began his blessings. It was a very formal speech, most of it in Latin. I stopped listening and thought about where we would live. If Sophie moved to Menton where Richard had his practice, what would happen to Les Lianes? Would I live there alone?

"He's not coming," Jules said.

"How do you know?" I asked.

"Haven't you been listening?"

Matisse, too ill to attend the ceremony, had written a note for the Bishop to read. Matisse presented the chapel to the Bishop and to the residents of the village of Vence. He excused the chapel's faults, and in spite of all its imperfections, called the chapel his masterpiece.

He asked the people of Vence and his friends on the Riviera to accept his masterpiece.

A few more people spoke and then we were invited to view Matisse's work.

The line to see the interior of the chapel formed, but it moved very slowly.

Jules wasn't happy. "Too many people," he said.

The chapel was the most extraordinary thing I had ever seen. It was exactly the opposite of every other church I had ever been in. Like comparing Paris to Nice. One was dark and heavy, old and most likely dirty. This chapel was white and light. The stained glass windows were blue and yellow with bits of green. Even the floor was white and so clean that the windows reflected the colors like mirrors.

The crowds were silent, not because it was a place of worship but because it was so beautiful. It was a happy place, not at all gloomy. In a place like that, one felt God's presence to be positive, not repressive.

Grandfather asked several times about Sophie. I told him not to worry.

He didn't seem worried, just wondering whether or not she would come.

I had followed Jules outside, but went back inside when a man came out to tell me that Grandfather wasn't feeling well. I found Grandfather sitting on one of the chairs. One of the Sisters had a fan and she moved it around him to create some air.

It was not a particularly warm night and Grandfather was not the fainting kind.

"I'm fine," Grandfather said and told me not to fuss.

Grandfather asked the woman for a glass of water and told me

I should go out and assure Hilda and Jules that there was no cause to worry.

"Sophie hasn't shown up, has she?"

"Don't worry about Sophie," I said. "Take care of yourself."

I didn't think Grandfather was in danger, so I did as he told me.

A few minutes later, he came out and Hilda suggested we leave if Grandfather wasn't feeling well.

The night was not as eventful as I had hoped.

Grandfather and Hilda fell asleep on the way home.

Jules and I talked about the chapel. He seemed unhappy but denied it when I asked him why.

"It is a masterpiece," I said.

"I'm not used to sharing Matisse with everyone," Jules said.

"But you do," I said. "Every day. People all over the world admire his works."

"But he's mine," Jules said. "I live here with him. I see the same things he does. I know how he feels."

"And yet you don't really know him," I said.

"I don't."

"You saved Coppi's life." I pointed out. "That must make you feel good."

"He won the stage, but not the Giro."

"At least he finished," I said. "Without you, he might have been killed."

"Your imagination is as active as mine, Agnes."

It didn't feel like a compliment, but I tried to take it as one. I needed something positive from him.

I don't know what time it was when Sophie got home, but I woke when I heard her on the steps. She was barefoot. I could hear her heels smacking against the floorboards.

I had fallen asleep in her room and when she came in, I clicked on the light. She squinted and threw a scarf over the lampshade to dim the light.

"What happened?" I said

"We got lost," she whispered.

She didn't have to lie to me. "You did not," I said. "But that's what Grandfather thinks."

"Good." She sat beside me.

"Did he ask you to marry him?"

She stretched out on the bed without taking off her dress. "Why would you think that?"

"It was that kind of night," I said. It had been in the beginning. But something had happened to the night's potential.

"He did not ask me to marry him."

"Why didn't you come to Vence?" I asked.

"I guess we wanted to be alone," she said.

"Is everything all right?" I asked.

"It's not great," she said.

She put her head forward; the base of her neck was pale, thin white hairs stood on end. She ran her hands through her chignon, messing it completely. A few of her hairpins fell to the floor and I picked out the rest until her hair was loose and hung down over her shoulders.

"What is it?"

"Let's not talk right now," Sophie said. She turned and crawled under the covers, without washing or changing out of her dress. She clicked off the light and in a minute I heard her breathing as if asleep. I don't know if she was, but I didn't have any desire to talk either.

That night marked the end of something and I was sad, before I really understood what it was that was gone.

I sat in the chair by her bed and fretted until I saw the pale strip of gray light the sky. Then I went downstairs and waited with Cook for the dairyman.

Chapter Eight

*T*he storm clouds came from the north and hung heavy and gray over the mountains. It rained for three days in a row and the coast was gloomy, the air thick with humidity.

"Do you know what they say about Coppi?" Jules asked.

We had spent the week with nothing to do in one of the small windowless cafés in Monte Carlo. The radio played all day long and gave us something to listen to. It passed the time.

The yellow tiles were slick; the owner had just washed the floors. His wife was behind the bar making our coffee. We were the only ones seated. Everyone else stood at the bar. Jules read the newspaper, but looked up when I told him yes. "I probably do," I said.

"You do what?" he asked.

"I probably know what you're going to tell me about Coppi. I figure I know as much as anyone else about Fausto Coppi," I said. I had been a good student and had done well in my lessons.

"I doubt that," he said.

"So tell me what you want to tell me and then I'll know."

"They say that when he finishes a day's stage, he makes his manager and trainers carry him into the hotel. He doesn't want to waste the energy of walking. They carry him to bed. Cradled in their arms like a baby."

Coppi was that fanatical about racing. Nothing else mattered to him. He was so focused on winning and racing, he calculated the meals and calories, and worried about the number of minutes he slept.

"That's what it takes to win," Jules said and he sighed. "It's depressing."

"But why should that depress you?" I asked.

"Most days it doesn't," Jules said. "Then on others it does, when I think of how little I achieve. How success is so far away, I get the blues."

I understood.

"I hate the rain, the gray skies," Jules complained. "It reminds me of my youth."

"Did it rain a lot in Marseilles?"

"How should I know?" Jules said, and stubbed out his cigarette in the already full ashtray.

"Because that's where you grew up."

He rubbed his eyes with both fists until they were red.

"Agnes, I don't want to talk about myself. I'm not interesting. I'm the least interesting person I know."

"I think you're interesting," I said. But he was not being interesting that day. In fact, he hadn't been interesting since the night of the consecration ceremony. Everything seemed to put him in a sour mood. "What's wrong?"

"My heart hurts," he said. "My liver hurts."

"You sound like an old person."

"That's right. I'm old and infirm. Nothing to do but end it all."

"Why are you talking like this?"

"Because," Jules said. "The summer is already well underway and I am no closer to my goal than I was when I started."

"That's true," I said.

"I haven't gotten anywhere on my road to greatness."

I was impatient. "What about me?" I asked. "Do you think I've made any progress on my goal?"

"I don't know," Jules said. "I haven't the slightest idea what your goal is." He reminded me that I had never told him. "Tell me and maybe I could help you."

"You could help," I said.

"Then let me," Jules said. "I'd be very happy. Then the two of you, the sisters Rouart, can triumph over the loser, Monsieur Agard."

"All right," I said.

"You want me to help you?"

"Oh yes," I sighed. My words were right there. I was going to tell him the truth. I leaned close to him and put my face to his. My cheek laid against his and I breathed in the aroma of Jules.

"What are you doing?" he asked.

I blushed. Had he not pulled away, I might have put my lips to his.

Jules stood up and went to the door to check on the weather. "We might as well be in the north," Jules sighed and went over to the window. "What good is it to us to be on the coast if all it's going to do is storm?"

"I have an idea," I announced. I went up and stood next to him. I wanted to be near him. Had he been listening I'm sure he could have heard my desire. It was loud, impatient, and desperately agitated by his lethargy.

"Really?" Jules asked.

"I think we should write a letter to Coppi," I said. "We should invite him out to dinner or lunch or for a day's excursion."

"Write him a letter."

I planned quickly. I went back to the table. I took my pen and began scribbling words down. "We can remind him of the day in the village above San Remo."

Jules sighed. "He gets thousands of letters every day. Ours won't mean anything to him."

"All right," I said. I had to do something. I couldn't let everything I had worked for fade into the gloom of a rainy Riviera afternoon. I had to save my relationship with Jules.

"Let's go to the Hotel Regina," I said.

"I'm not in the mood."

"But today will be different. Today we will meet him."

"But how will today be any different?" Jules asked. "We've been there a dozen times and haven't caught a glimpse of him. The staff is suspicious and will probably throw us out just as they do every other time."

The hotel staff was unusually protective of Matisse's privacy and when we asked questions, the front desk clerk answered vaguely as if he didn't quite know whether or not Matisse was actually living there again.

"I have a plan," I announced and then I immediately began thinking up one.

"What can we do that we haven't done before?"

He hesitated but finally agreed to a trip into Nice. The streets near the old port and promenade were crowded with tourists. It was the beginning of the high season—a time when all the people from Paris came to the south for the vacation. We drove up into Cimiez and parked outside the hotel.

"Wait here," I told Jules. "I'll be right back."

"You're going in alone?" he smiled. I amused him with my determination.

"Not to worry," I said. "I'm fully aware of what the landscape demands."

I went in and marched right up to the waiter who was setting the inside tables for lunch. The rain was too heavy for any outdoor service.

I did my best Sophie imitation. "Is it true that Matisse lives here in this hotel?" I asked and smiled widely at him.

"Who wants to know?" he said and I knew I had found what I wanted.

I looked around, then leaned in and whispered. "A very nosy girl."

He touched the tip of my nose. "And that's you?

"That's me," I said.

"You're looking for Matisse?"

"I'd like to see him."

"You would? Why?"

"Because," I said, and, thought quickly. "Because my older brother is dying," I said. I was desperate and realized the truth wasn't going to get me anywhere.

The waiter was busy, but he listened to my story of my very ill brother who had one wish. "It won't be long," I said.

"He's that ill?"

"Extremely ill."

"And he wants to see Matisse?" the waiter asked.

"That's all he wants," I said. "Just to see Matisse."

"Where's your brother now?"

"Outside," I said, and nodded towards the front of the hotel.

"In the rain?" the waiter asked. "You left your sick brother out there in the storm?"

I nodded, but didn't mention the car. The black Cadillac didn't fit with my story.

The waiter informed me that it was true. Matisse was living in one of the large studio apartments on the top floor. He worked in seclusion. No one was ever to interrupt him for any reason. He sat at a table outside, but very close to the doors where it was shaded and where the waiters attended him as quickly as they could. He drank a glass of beer and ate an omelet. Then he had a coffee and something sweet. The waiters then helped him back up to his room.

The waiter told me I could bring my brother in. "Sit there," he said, and pointed to the table closest to the one where Matisse lunched.

I went out and got Jules. I told him what I had learned.

"He eats lunch there every day?"

"That's what I was told."

"But why haven't we ever seen him?"

"He hides," I explained. "The waiter told me he usually wears a straw hat with a wide brim. You can't see his face and he doesn't speak to anyone."

Jules nodded. "Very good, Agnes," he said.

We went in and sat at the designated table. The bar was warm and smelled of cigarettes and wet clothes. It was pleasant and I thought the afternoon would turn in our favor.

We waited.

We drank coffee and waited some more.

The waiter assured me Matisse was coming down. "He probably got up late because of the rain, but don't worry, he'll come. He's very punctual. His days do not vary."

The rain fell. The umbrellas had been taken in and stacked against the inside wall. Jules hung his head and I saw the waiter watching him carefully.

The lunch hour passed. A number of people dined, but Matisse did not come down.

The waiter was insistent. "He'll be here."

But he didn't come.

The day had lost all purpose and I think Jules was trying to work up the energy to drive me home.

"I yearn for fame, but understand that I am not destined for greatness."

"But you're still young," I said. "Things might change."

"I dabble at things," he said. "But I don't have the talent for anyone to look at my work. No one will know my name when I die."

I found this tragic and told him so.

"You're right," Jules agreed. "It is tragic."

"But can't you do something?"

"It's too late," Jules said. "I am destined to be a nobody."

It was painful to see him so down. "You talk like your life is over," I said.

"I am the lanterne rouge."

The red light, the last man to finish the race.

Jules shook his head. "No. I'm not even as good as the lanterne rouge. I'm not even in the race."

I don't know how long the policemen had been standing around Jules' car, but when I looked up, there they were grouped around the front end, looking at the identification numbers.

They approached the hotel and a few minutes later walked into the bar area.

"Jules Agard?" they spoke as they approached the table.

Jules was taken by surprise. He spun around, knocking his spoon to the floor. Mathilde had once warned me that spoons on the floor were bad luck.

"I'm Jules Agard," he said. He looked worried. "Are you here about my mother?"

"Your mother?" they said. "No."

"What's wrong?" Jules said. He held his billfold as if they meant to look at his papers. They motioned that he could put that away.

"We were hoping we could talk to you." They were very polite. "When you finish your lunch. There's no rush."

"May I ask why?" Jules said.

"It's a personal matter," they said.

"Concerning me?"

"Yes," they said. "That's why we'd like to talk to you."

We had finished our coffees. There was no reason to wait.

Jules put some francs on the white saucer and the waiter came by to rip the chit in half.

I leaned over and whispered to the waiter. "If you see Matisse, tell him we'll be here tomorrow."

"And who shall I say called for him?" the waiter asked.

I smiled. "Tell him," I said, thinking carefully. "Tell him it was two residents of the Riviera who would like to discuss his work with him."

The waiter nodded. "And shall I mention you received a police escort away from the hotel?"

"Maybe it would be best to leave that part out."

"I think that's wise," the waiter said.

The policemen and Jules waited for me by the door, then all of us stepped out into the wet afternoon. The storm had gotten worse and the rain came down in sheets from the heavy skies.

The police station was in the old part of Nice. The streets were heavy with traffic because of the rain. On days when people could not walk on the promenades or stroll the flower and fruit markets, everyone got in their cars and bottled up the streets.

Once in the station, they offered us towels and coffee and seemed genuinely concerned about our comfort.

"I think it's going to be okay," I whispered to Jules when the one policeman went to fetch me some milk for the coffee.

He took the towel and wrapped it around his neck. "What is?" he asked.

"I think we're here as witnesses, not as potential criminals."

"What makes you think that?"

"Would they treat us so well if they suspected us of a major crime?"

"This isn't part of your scandals, is it?" Jules asked.

"They wanted to talk to you, not me," I reminded him. The older policeman had offered to take me home, but I had refused. "Jules is my friend," I told him. "I can't leave him here alone."

"He'll hardly be alone," the policeman assured me.

"I'm a loyal friend," I said. "He may need my help."

The other one agreed. "What's the difference. Let her stay."

They came back with a tiny pitcher of cream and I poured it in my coffee. The coffee was very hot and I sipped slowly trying to make it last.

They were very businesslike and got right to the point.

"You were at the opening of the Matisse chapel in Vence this week."

"For the consecration?" I asked.

They nodded.

"We were," I said. "We both were."

"Agnes," Jules said. "Maybe you'd let me answer every other question?"

"By all means," I said. "Talk your head off."

They asked Jules about his visit that night. What he did, where he stood, what he saw.

"Why do you want to know all this?" I asked.

"Something was stolen from the chapel that night," they explained. "Candlesticks."

"And you think I'm responsible?" Jules said. He had spilled some coffee on his shirt; a dark-brown wet stain circled right below his collarbone.

I was quiet as I remembered what Jules had said the night we took Grandfather to tea at Hilda Koch's house. He had been quite open in his adoration of the sketch. He desired it. He had told me so himself. I remembered his words: that given a choice, he would have stolen the Matisse.

The policemen assured us that they were talking to everyone who had attended the ceremony. They had the book, the one we had signed as we left the chapel. They were going through all the names, most had given addresses and they were asking everyone for any information or help. They had gone to Jules' apartment and the landlord told them about the car. They had been at the hotel, not to see Jules, but to speak with Matisse.

"It was just our luck we saw your car there," they said. Though I wondered if it didn't make us more suspicious.

"I don't remember the candlesticks," Jules said. Neither did I, but I didn't say that as I didn't want them to think we were being deliberately vague about objects we were supposed to have admired.

"They're valuable. A part of what the artist wanted to complete the total picture."

Jules nodded. "I'm surprised anyone would do anything to ruin Matisse's masterpiece."

Jules and I didn't actually talk about money, but there were days when he seemed to have some; days when he had none. I wasn't sure how he got more. Where did it come from?

They explained that it was a curious theft. The people at the consecration ceremony were respected members of the community; many had helped raise money for the completion of the chapel, and so it was odd that someone would try and sabotage the chapel on the night it was officially opened.

After what I thought was a very pleasant interview, we were told that we could leave.

*T*he rain had stopped, but when I suggested a visit to the beach, Jules said he was tired. "Besides, the chairs will be all wet."

"We can wipe them off," I said. "They have towels."

He determined it too dreary and said it was time for him to take me home.

A slow-moving piece of farm machinery drove in front of us and the trip back to Les Lianes took much longer than it should have. We were both silent, each of us lost in thought.

"You didn't take the candlesticks, did you?" I asked.

"I'm not a thief," Jules answered.

"I didn't think so," I said.

"Then why did you ask?"

"Because I could understand if you did," I said. And I did. I didn't think it wrong.

"Because you might have wanted something of his," I said.

"I don't think Matisse made the candlesticks," Jules mused. "But either way, I wouldn't take them. To what end?"

I reminded him how much he had liked Hilda Koch's sketch. The pencil lines on the paper. The girl sitting on the chair, the breeze blowing the curtain open to show the sea behind her.

"It's beautiful," Jules said. "But I didn't steal that either. I think you're missing the point. I don't want what they have. I don't cherish their things. I cherish them. There's a world of difference."

"Oh," I said.

I ate dinner alone. Grandfather was with Hilda. I guessed that Sophie was still in town with Richard.

I ate quickly, then brought my plate into the kitchen and set it in the tub of water where the pots were soaking.

Mathilde was setting up the large table to do her ironing. She had wrapped a thick cloth around one end of the table. In the basket were her things—the napkins and sheets from her trousseau.

She was humming. She nodded. I said hello and she said something I didn't understand. I thought it most likely that she was talking to herself. I let it go, but then she repeated it. Louder, clearly intended for me to hear.

"What's that?" I asked.

"Veules-les-Roses," she said.

"What's that?"

"That's the name of the village where I grew up," Mathilde said.

"Has someone else drowned there?" I asked.

"Not that I know of," Mathilde said.

"Are you going back?" I asked.

"It's very small," she said. "Less than a thousand people live there."

"I'm sure it's very nice," I told her. Her apron was stained with tomato seeds. They were grouped in a tight design that from far away might look like a flower.

"Do you know the smallest river in all of France runs through our village?"

"I did not," I said.

"It starts in the middle of town and goes right out to the sea. Three kilometers. That's interesting, isn't it."

"Maybe," I told her. "I'm sure someone might find it interesting, but I don't."

"Your friend," Mathilde said, and the words hung in the air. She shrugged as if she didn't know how to finish the rest of her sentence.

"What friend?" I asked. "Which one are you talking about?"

"Listen to you," Mathilde said. "Like you have so many you don't know who I'm talking about."

It was true. Friends were not something I had been collecting that summer.

"You have one friend," she informed me. "And that's who I'm talking about." She moved around the table, brushing imaginary crumbs from the surface. I wished fervently for a whole loaf of stale bread. I would rip it into tiny bits and scatter them about. At least that way her movements wouldn't be as wasted as her words.

That humming. An odd tune that wasn't a song, but merely a chance to show me she was happy.

"He hasn't changed," Mathilde sighed.

I listened, but wasn't looking at her. My friendship with Jules was not her business. He was mine, at least as far as I was concerned, and I did not have to share him with anybody. I sat down.

"Not in all these years. He hasn't changed one bit. He's exactly like he used to be."

She crossed to the bucket to dump her apron of whatever it was that she thought she had collected. Her slippers shuffled across the tiles like a fat old woman who didn't have the strength to lift her legs.

"Jules Agard."

I had never told Mathilde his last name. She either discovered this on her own, or she was speaking the truth. I preferred to think Sophie had told her.

"Little skinny Jules Agard," she said. She carried the plates into the kitchen.

I forced myself into silence. "Don't give her what she wants," I chanted in my head. *She's trying to goad you. Teasing you. She and Sophie must have been up all night sharing secrets. She's pretending to know things because she wants to upset you.*

Mathilde sat across from me as if the two of us were having an enjoyable conversation. "When we were kids, he was like a brother to me," she said. I couldn't help myself. I looked up. She was watching me intently—checking for any surprise on my face.

"Is that right?" I asked. How could she be speaking the truth? Why would she and Sophie have discussed Jules? Why did he interest Mathilde?

"It is," Mathilde said. "We used to call him monkey-face. Ask him if he remembers. Little monkey-face."

The sweat on the back of my knees ran down my legs. He had told me of his childhood nickname. But had he told Sophie too?

"His parents were the caretakers at the largest house in our village. An apple farm."

"In Normandy?" I asked. Jules had never mentioned Normandy. I would have remembered that geographical reference. He was a man of the south, a resident of the Riviera. Marseille, Cannes, Monte Carlo, Nice. He knew these places like someone who had grown up there. He spoke with the nasality of someone from the South. He knew every road, every café, every roadside turnout. He knew where to see the best sunsets, were to watch the thunderstorms. He knew the buildings where Matisse had lived in the 1920s, where he had moved in the '30s. He knew the area as if he had lived there his entire life.

"Apple orchards are what makes money where I come from. The family his parents worked for had one of the largest orchards in the region."

My stomach ached. She was not making this up. Mathilde was quirky—skittish and full of strange fears and odd beliefs—but she was not a liar.

"His father's dead," she said. "That's how he got the car. It belonged to the man they cared for. He willed them some money and the car. That's how they came here."

"Oh?" was all I could manage.

"Oh yes," she continued. "They couldn't stay in the village. Not with so few people. Everyone knew who they were. Their status had changed. It wasn't a lot of money, but it was more than anyone else had so they came here after his father died." Mathilde was gloating. She leaned over the table and pressed her face near mine. She smelled of our dinner, onions and barley along with the stale smell of perfume against skin that was not bathed every day. I knew she feared the water, feared that it would erase years from her life. She was only a few years older than I was, but I hated her old-fashioned superstitions, her fears. And most of all I hated how she thought she had something over on me.

I got up from the table and went upstairs. I had heard enough for one night.

I decided not to confront Jules with what Mathilde had told me. I dreaded what he would say and the easiest way not to hear his response was to keep quiet. I pretended that nothing had changed.

But Mathilde wouldn't leave it alone. "Did you ask Jules about Veules-les-Roses?"

"I forgot," I said. I had thought of nothing else since she told me everything.

Mathilde became thoughtful. "I don't know why it matters. He wouldn't want to see me. I wasn't anybody important. My parents worked the fields in the summer. He would be ashamed to be seen with someone like me."

I picked through the things in her basket.

"He would be embarrassed to see me again," Mathilde said. "He's obviously a changed man."

I nodded in agreement. "Jules doesn't care for the past. The present is the only thing that matters."

"Is that right?" she asked.

"It's what he says." I felt as if I was quoting God, the words were so sacred to me.

"We had a good childhood," she said. "It wasn't bad. I don't think he'll mind being reminded of it."

"I can't say what he'll think."

She had an odd expression on her face. "You probably won't ever tell him," she said. "If I know you, you won't say a word."

"That's not true," I said. "Of course I'm going tell him about you," I said. I regretted it as soon as I said it.

On one hand, I wanted to tell Jules everything Mathilde had told me. All the details of his childhood in Normandy. I wanted to give him the chance to refute it. To provide me with some explanation as to why she knew things about him. I wanted him to deny her story. On the other hand, I wanted to forget the whole turn of events. I wanted to erase what Mathilde had told me. How easy it would be to go back to before she had told me she knew Jules.

But it weighed too heavily on my mind. The next time he came, I told him I had something to discuss with him.

"What's that, little one?" Jules walked up the steps and sat beside me. "You don't look so good."

I didn't know how to begin, so I simply said her name. "Mathilde Guillebaud."

He was surprised. "Who?"

I said it again.

This time he heard and repeated it after me. "Mathilde Guillebaud? Do you know her?"

"I do," I said. "I wish I didn't, but I do."

"How do you know her?" he asked.

"She's our maid."

"Is it the same one? The one I know?" Jules asked. "The one from Veules-les-Roses?"

"You tell me," I said. "I wasn't there."

"It must be," Jules said. "How many Mathilde Guillebaud's can there be in the world?"

He was not at all embarrassed. Not at all ashamed that in acknowledging Mathilde, he had admitted himself to be a liar.

"I would like to see her."

"Now?" I asked.

"If she's not busy," Jules said.

"Don't forget that today is the day we talk to Matisse," I said. "It's a day that could change your life forever."

He followed me around back to the kitchen and when he saw Mathilde he embraced her, then gave a cry of delight.

"You," he said. "It is you."

"It's me," Mathilde said. Her face was bright red and she wiped her mouth with the back of her hand.

"You look exactly the same," Jules said. "You haven't changed a bit."

"So do you," Mathilde said.

"You're in service now." He touched her skirt and she slapped his hand away as if he was flirting with her.

"I am," she said. "It's a respectable job."

"How did you come here?"

"I came with the family," Mathilde said. "Didn't the girl tell you?"

"I have a name," I said. "I think you know it." But they were too engrossed in each other and no one paid me any attention.

Jules talked to her exactly as he talked to me. "Isn't it marvelous here?"

"Where?" Mathilde looked around. "You like the kitchen? You can have it. I'm tired of it."

"The south. The Riviera. The entire Côte d'Azur. Isn't it lovely?"

"I guess so."

"What do you mean you guess so? It's beautiful."

"I don't know about that. What I see most often are the walls of this house."

"It's a grand house."

"Perhaps it is."

I resented their conversation, but neither paid attention to my protest that it was time Jules and I got going. We were wasting the day inside the villa. The afternoon rain would meet us before we even had a chance to enjoy the sunshine.

"You'll have to let me change that," Jules said. "It's wonderful. The most wonderful place in the world. I love it here."

Mathilde rolled her eyes and giggled.

"Those are not the words I'd use to describe this place. The bugs and the animals. The winds are too strong when they come off the mountains."

Jules wouldn't stop grinning. "You haven't changed. You haven't changed a bit."

I wanted Jules to find Mathilde ridiculous and bothersome.

"Come see my mother. She would love to see a face from the old days."

"I will," Mathilde promised.

He leaned forward and hugged her again. I didn't think there had to be so much physical contact. They were old friends. He could leave it at that. Certainly they didn't have to hug every time one of them said something. She was a silly girl but his happiness was unmistakable and therefore confusing.

They talked a few more minutes, giving me no choice but to tell Jules we had to go. "Remember. It's our day to see Matisse." We had decided that this was the day when we would see him having his lunch. It was to be our day to see and talk to the great man.

Jules smiled. "Patience is a virtue, Agnes."

Mathilde giggled. "You can tell her that twice," she said. "It's something she needs to hear."

I shot her a look, but Jules laughed, which made me angrier. I wasn't impatient with most people. Only with Mathilde.

Finally Jules was ready to go.

I got in the car and slammed the door. "Maybe you could help me understand what just happened in there."

He had a grin on his face as wide as the ocean. His white teeth and thin lips were just so pleased with themselves. "Little Mathilde. She was always a funny-looking little girl."

"Some things don't change," I mumbled.

"I remember her as a little girl with no front teeth," Jules said. "She lost them early and they took years to grow in."

"How is it that you're suddenly from Normandy?" I asked.

"It's not sudden. It's where I'm from," he said. "It's where I've always been from."

"It's certainly news to me."

"Is it?" he asked.

"What happened to Marseille?" I asked. "The butcher's shop? The little bicycle and the deliveries of cheese and meat?"

"That's my Coppi fantasy," Jules said. "I like to make my childhood as close to his as possible."

"What about being a lifelong resident of the Riviera?" I asked.

"My parents were caretakers on an apple farm up in Normandy," he said. "They took care of the rich family in my childhood village. Didn't Mathilde tell you?"

"She tells me a lot of things, most of which I don't pay attention to. She's not a bright girl."

"She was always fun," Jules said.

"I guess that's okay," I said. "If you like that sort of thing."

"What's wrong with you?" he said. "What's made you so cross?"

"I've told you about Mathilde," I said. "She's the one who's afraid of everything. Animals, bees, shadows, ghosts, anything that moves. She's a ninny."

"She was always like that," Jules said. "I remember she hated the water. She was afraid of the ocean, which was silly because the Atlantic dominated our village."

"I thought you didn't like talking of the past."

"I don't normally," Jules said.

"Seeing Mathilde has changed that?"

He spoke of his parents, of growing up in the farmhouse where his parents were the caretakers. "The house was filled with old people. Sick old people who did nothing but talk about their ailments and how much better things were before. Before they got old. It was tiresome. I vowed I wouldn't do it. Never, I promised myself. I heard my parents do it. All my relatives. It's the thing I hate most in people."

"Then what was all that in the kitchen?" I asked.

"Mathilde and I are young," he said. "We're not boring old people. We didn't talk about illnesses or how great our lives were before the war."

I told him I didn't see much of a difference.

"Yesterday is not important," Jules said. "Living in the present makes the future seem real and possible. Life moves forward. That's how I want to live it."

If this were true then maybe I had nothing to worry about. Maybe it had been an act. If he was someone who didn't care about what happened, then he wouldn't care about Mathilde.

But now I didn't know what to believe. I asked Jules if he had made up everything he told me.

"Most of it," Jules said.

"Why?"

"It's a habit of mine."

"All of it?"

"Anything that wasn't true, I made up."

"The woman in the casino," I asked. "Was that your mother?"

"Yes," Jules said. "But I didn't lie about that. I distinctly recall telling you the truth, but you wouldn't hear of it. If I remember correctly, you said it was impossible."

"Why?" I asked.

"Why is she my mother?" Jules asked. "I'm not sure I had anything to do with that. Fate probably played a role there."

"Why did you lie?" I really wanted to know why had he lied to me.

"I wouldn't call it lying."

"I do," I said. "Lying is when you don't tell the truth. That's what you did."

"I've embellished certain details," Jules said. "My desire to be like Coppi sometimes overwhelms me."

Things were out of control. Discussing it seemed pointless, but I had to. "It's a terrible habit," I said. "It's damaging."

"Doesn't everyone?" Jules asked. "Imagine different pasts? Different scenarios of our childhoods?"

"Everyone has fantasies," I said. "But not every one parades them like they are the truth."

I was still trying to pout, which was impossible, as Jules didn't seem to notice or care about my anger. He acted as if I had misplaced my lipstick or forgotten to the buy bread for dinner.

But what good would anger do?

I pretended that Jules had not lied to me about anything important. I thought it over carefully. He was embarrassed by his humble upbringing, ashamed to tell me that his parents had been servants. I knew he had aspirations of greatness; this was something he had bragged to me about. I debated the issue of loss and lies and came to the conclusion that Jules was an entertainer. It was one of the things he did best.

In his own words, the landscape of the area demanded entertainment. That's how I reasoned his betrayal. He had done it for my benefit.

I forgave him for lying about Normandy. I had a harder time forgiving him for knowing Mathilde. I could not forgive him for the attention he paid Mathilde but I thought if I ignored it, it would go away. Jules was, after all, a man who did not care to talk about the past; I couldn't imagine him reliving it with Mathilde every time they talked. Jules had to grow tired of her. It was probably only a matter of days. I forced myself to be patient, but it wasn't easy.

Chapter Nine

*G*randfather was the one who told me about Fausto Coppi's brother.

"Your friend had some bad luck today," Grandfather said. He came out to the garden and found me pretending to read. The clouds were blocking the sun and it was cold. I had a blanket wrapped around my legs and felt like an invalid, like one of the consumptives I had seen in photographs of the spas in the Alps—lines of sick wrapped up in tight cocoons, their faces turned towards the sun.

"Jules?" I sat up and pushed the blankets from around my legs. "What happened? What happened to him?"

"Jules who?"

"You know who Jules is, Grandfather," I said. "Is something wrong with him?"

"I'm talking about the Italian racer," Grandfather said. He put out his cigarette and tossed the end into the garden. He and Sophie shared this habit and I worried about fires.

"Coppi?" I asked.

"That's right," Grandfather said. "There's been an accident."

"Is he hurt?"

"They don't know all the details," he explained. "But someone's been hurt."

We went inside and had to wait almost an hour to hear the sporting news.

The news was not good.

Fausto Coppi and his younger brother, Serse, had been racing the Giro del Piemonte, a race Fausto was using as a warm-up for the Tour de France. It was an easier ride and he and his brother were coasting in towards the finish line, when Serse bumped into another rider and fell from his bike.

He got up immediately and seemed fine. He got back on his bike and finished the race.

A few hours later, he began complaining of pains. The pain grew worse and he was rushed to the hospital. That's all they knew. Serse Coppi was in the hospital and we waited for news.

Grandfather turned the radio up louder. We sat there most of the night.

"He must be really hurt," Grandfather said. "They aren't reporting a thing. If he were fine, they would have said something. But to say nothing is bad."

He wasn't hurt. He was dead. He died in the Italian hospital five hours after falling off his bicycle.

Fausto Coppi was devastated. Serse was not only his beloved brother, he was his teammate and training partner.

There were only ten days until the start of the Tour de France.

*J*ules called Serse's death the end of Coppi. "He's finished."

"You don't know. He could take his grief and turn it around. He could win the Tour. He could ride down the Champs-Élysées a winner. You'll be sorry then."

It's not going to happen," Jules said.

"You have a crystal ball into the future?" I asked. "Did a fortune-teller tell you who's going to win the Tour?"

"His luck has run out," Jules said. "He had it for awhile. He turned the world's head towards him. But now it's over."

I know we were talking about an Italian bicycle racer, but I couldn't help but feel that Jules was talking about himself. The joy had drained from our days. I didn't think Jules was having fun anymore. Our days felt heavy, as if we weren't doing anything but counting off the hours.

Jules said he needed a break. "Some time off," he said.

"Time off from me?" I asked.

"Just from going to the beach every day," Jules said. "I need to see to some things."

"Because of Coppi?" I asked.

He sighed heavily.

"Is that why you don't want to see me?" I asked.

"I want to see you," Jules said. "I've got to spend some time looking for a job. A few days. That's all. Don't make it seem like the end of the world."

I couldn't believe it didn't have anything to do with me.

A few days later, I heard Jules' car tires moving across the gravel. It was early evening, a time when Jules did not normally stop by the villa. I leaned out the window. My heart healed immediately when I saw the car coming slowly up to the villa. I began to wave wildly. "Up here. Up here," I said, but the motor was too loud and he couldn't hear. I ran downstairs.

Then Mathilde came from the other side of the house. "Jules," she said. "Here you are."

I felt like a fool. The gravel stones bit into my bare feet.

They were dressed to go out. Jules wore a jacket. Mathilde wore a dress, stockings, and a pair of Sophie's shoes.

"Does Sophie know you've taken her shoes?" I asked.

Mathilde smiled. I didn't know what that meant. She wore makeup. Red lipstick and eye shadow that made her eyes look as if they were going to spring out of her head.

If she thought I wasn't going to tell Sophie about the shoes, she was wrong.

"Have fun tonight, little one," Mathilde said.

Jules got out of the car. "Good evening, Agnes," Jules waved. "Are you feeling better?"

"I didn't know I was sick," I said.

We stood there looking at each other. Then Jules said it was time they got going.

He helped Mathilde in the car.

Jules told me he'd see me soon.

"When?" I said.

"Real soon." He went around the car and fiddled with the side mirror, oblivious that I was having trouble breathing. The air around me was dark and my stomach raced with fear and disbelief. I felt like he had kicked me, then wished he had. It would have been less painful.

Mathilde sat in my seat as if it belonged to her.

I seethed.

"Who knows?" she said. "I may get to use my trousseau sooner than I imagined."

She had nerve.

Jules started the car and drove off. When he got to the gates, he honked twice. The horn was high-pitched and friendly. Mathilde turned and looked at me. She waved wildly, a huge smile across her too-red lips.

Oh how I hated her. I picked up a handful of stone gravel and threw it at the car. I missed, but I did it again—another handful, and another, and another—I dug into the ground, my nails stinging and when I could no longer hear the sound of the car's engine, I threw the rocks at my own legs. Handful after handful until the entire patch of drive looked as if wild dogs had been trampling through. My nails were black with dirt, my face streaked with tears.

Mathilde was evil. She was using her past to seduce Jules. He who hated the past, claimed to have no use for what happened before, was suddenly romancing a girl from his youth.

It was Mathilde's fault. She had ruined everything. My goal to get Jules to love me was futile. She had stolen him from me. I could not let her get away with these sorts of venomous actions.

I vowed revenge.

I wanted her gone.

I acted quickly. That night, when everyone was asleep, I sneaked down to Grandfather's study. It was midnight. The household slept. Grandfather was there asleep on the couch. I took his billfold from the top drawer of his desk. The wood creaked as I tried to shut it.

I was going to shame Mathilde into leaving.

Grandfather, a meticulous man, discovered the missing billfold early the next morning. By the time I came down, he was upset and was pacing the floor of his study. His voice filled the house.

"Who would have guessed it?" he said. "The Dutch haven't been right in centuries."

"They haven't?" I asked.

"Of course not," he said. "Look what a mess they made of Indonesia. Fools."

I didn't know that history. He would have explained it if I asked, so I didn't.

"Hilda was right; there are thieves among us," he yelled. He circled around himself in the small room, moving books and newspapers, checking everywhere for his billfold. "They come in right while you're sleeping and help themselves to your things."

"Really?" I asked. "What's missing?" I heard footfalls. Cook and Mathilde were aware that something was wrong. It was only a matter of time before one of them put her ear to the door.

"My billfold is gone."

"I know who did it," I said.

Grandfather took my hand. I thought he was going to kiss it, but he only squeezed it. "Good. I'm glad."

He did not ask me to identify the culprit. Instead he complimented me on my interest in his affairs. "It's about time someone took some interest in my concerns."

"I can help," I said. "I think I know who did it."

I repeated that I knew who was to blame several times before Grandfather finally heard what I was saying.

"Mathilde," I said. "She was the one who took your billfold."

"The girl?"

"It must have been." I knew Mathilde heard my accusations. I wanted her to feel bad, to feel awful about her herself.

"Mathilde," I said.

"Why would she take my billfold?"

"Because she wanted the money," I suggested. "Maybe she needed it. I'm sure she's got her reasons."

"I don't think she'd steal from me."

"You don't know."

"How extraordinary. Do you really believe she'd do something like that?"

"I do," I said.

I heard Mathilde's cry of anguish, then the shuffle of her slippers as she moved down the hall to seek out Cook.

Grandfather found the money. I had suggested he might look in Mathilde's embroidery basket.

He was genuinely surprised to find it. "What's it doing here?" he asked.

"She took it," I said.

"But why would she steal from me?"

I wanted Mathilde gone.

"The police should be notified."

"Really?" Grandfather said.

"I think we should get them here."

Cook and Mathilde watched us in shock. It had been easy enough to slip the billfold into Mathilde's basket. She never put it away. It was always on the counter or on the table, in my way, just when I wanted to use the space it occupied.

Mathilde denied any knowledge of the missing billfold or money. "I wouldn't do a thing like that."

"The police will be very interested to hear that," I said.

"There's no need to get the police," Cook spoke up.

Mathilde was weeping and I stopped looking at her. She had made me weep and had gloated.

"Of course there is," I said.

Cook defended Mathilde. "She's a good girl. She's not a thief. She respects the house and the family. She wouldn't steal from you."

I told Grandfather that getting the police is what Father would do.

"He certainly would," Grandfather agreed. But he didn't volunteer to get them or tell me to do it.

Grandfather counted his money. I should have been cleverer about taking it out. Now that he had found the wallet, he didn't seem to care.

Mathilde, terrified and ashamed of being accused of doing something she would never have done, fled.

She took off on foot into the mountains.

Grandfather was furious at Cook for letting Mathilde leave.

"I don't really see that I could have stopped her, sir," Cook said. Cook was just as furious and the two of them began to fight like cats.

"But to let her go," Grandfather said.

"Maybe if you had treated her a bit better," Cook scolded him.

"She's a thief," Grandfather said. "You don't treat thieves with kindness. What's the point of that?"

"You don't know what happened," Cook said.

"I found the money in her things."

"She said she didn't take it," Cook said. "I believe her. She's not a liar."

"It certainly seems that she took it," Grandfather said.

"It seems that way, but maybe it wasn't."

They argued back and forth repeating themselves, neither one of them willing to listen to the other's opinion.

It was a relief to see Mathilde go. I had thought she would have put up more of a fight. I watched the flash of color as Mathilde walked up the mountain path. Soon she disappeared. I had taken walks up there myself. She would be afraid. The nettles were thick as the path narrowed, then finally disappeared altogether.

I had not planned on Sophie returning then. The bread truck had broken down and rather than wait until he could get someone to fix it, Sophie simply returned to the house.

Her flat shoes clicked against the foyer as she came running in to see the reason for the commotion. She startled me and though I tried to act as if nothing was wrong, she saw me standing in the hallway with a smile of satisfaction on my face, but nothing that warranted her anger.

"Why is everyone yelling?" she said.

"I guess they're upset," I said, then looked at her blankly as if I didn't really understand what everyone was doing either.

"You guess they're upset?"

I nodded and looked away. The sour expression on her face told me that she was not going to be nice.

"That's good, Agnes," Sophie said. "You've been here all morning? All this commotion and all you can tell me is that you think they're upset?"

"I know they're upset."

"Never mind," Sophie said. She was wearing too much perfume, the lavender trailed behind her as she ran to the kitchen. I waited a few minutes, then followed.

Sophie was not kind. She grabbed my arm and pulled me into the dry pantry and pressed my head against the stone wall. She whispered her threat. "Tell me. What is going on?"

"This isn't about me," I said. "I'm just trying to help."

"Why did Mathilde run away?"

"Because she stole Grandfather's money," I said. "She's guilty. Maybe she took enough to escape into Italy where she plans to live a life of leisure the rest of her days."

"You think Grandfather has that kind of money?"

I had never looked to see how much was in Grandfather's billfold.

"How should I know?"

"Because you do," Sophie said.

"Grandfather must be a wealthy man."

"There was a less than 100 francs in his billfold," Sophie said. She stared at me to see my reaction.

"I thought she stole the money," I said.

"No you didn't," she said.

"I did," I said. "Who else would have taken it?"

Sophie opened a jar of anchovies and ate one. Oil dripped down her chin and onto her white blouse where it would stain. She didn't seem to care. She took the back of her hand and wiped her mouth, then brushed it on her skirt as if wearing an apron.

The room was stuffy and warm. It smelled now of anchovies and Sophie's endless cigarette breath.

Sophie grabbed my arm and took my chin in her hands. I tried to turn away, but she was firm. "I recognize an act when I see one," she said.

"You think I took the money?" I asked.

"I think you know more than you're telling," Sophie said.

"Why would I lie about this?"

"I don't know why Mathilde bothers you, but I do know that she does."

I squirmed out of her grasp, but she had too much to say to let me off so easily.

"Mathilde is a poor girl who loved Mother. She hasn't had your privileges. And yet there's a friction between the two of you that shouldn't be there. It's so easy to be nice to someone like Mathilde."

But I didn't see it that way.

The people who lived down the road had a telephone and Sophie and Jules had a system they used to get in touch. She called the hotel next to his rooming house and for a small fee, the man who worked the desk would send someone to fetch Jules.

He came right away. I got up when I heard the car, but Sophie stopped me.

"No," she said. "I'm sending him to look for Mathilde. You can talk to him later."

"Can't I even say hello?"

"No," Sophie said. "She's got a huge head start. She's afraid and alone and I want him to find her."

I hadn't planned on this.

Sophie told me to go into Grandfather's study. "Wait there," she said. "And don't move. I want a full explanation."

Reluctantly I did as she told me. I stood at the patio doors. Straining to hear how she explained the situation to Jules. I couldn't hear much and didn't see Jules follow the path up the mountains to search for Mathilde.

*S*ophie came in to interrogate me. Her cheeks were pink with anger, her hair a mess of damp curls. She started by asking me to explain everything that had happened.

"Since when?" I asked.

"Let's start with breakfast," she said.

"I didn't have any," I said.

"Do you mean to be impossible or is this a game?" she said.

Right then Cook running down the hallway interrupted us. She was a big woman and her bulk surprised the objects on the table as she passed by—they shuddered as if frightened of falling.

"I haven't the slightest idea what's happening, but the police are here."

A dark car was parked under the mulberry trees.

Sophie asked me to explain.

"I don't know," I said.

"They just showed up?"

"I didn't invite them here if that's what you mean."

She asked the policemen in and told them to make themselves comfortable in the living room. They were the same ones who had questioned Jules and me at the station in Nice. But I thought this just a coincidence. I thought they had come because of Mathilde.

We said hello and chatted about the weather, then Sophie offered them something to drink, which they accepted.

"Come, Agnes," she said. "I need your help."

Now Grandfather was suddenly absent.

In the kitchen, Sophie flitted about. It was not her style to be frustrated, even with the police, and I told her to slow down. "You're going to break everything," I said.

She stopped and took a deep breath.

"If I didn't know better, I'd say you're guilty," I said.

She fixed a tray of olives and crackers. She counted out four glasses and took a bottle of white wine from the cupboard.

Before leaving, she turned to Cook and directed how things were to be.

"Father is not to know about this," she said.

"My lips are buttoned, sealed tight," Cook said. "I don't pry where it's not my business."

"Well, that's not entirely true," Sophie said.

"On this I won't say a word."

"I mean it," Sophie said. "I don't want Father to be told that the police were here."

"Why are they here?" I asked.

"You tell me," Sophie said. "You seem to be on friendly terms with them."

"I don't know," I asked.

Cook said the Riviera had stolen our sense. "There's too much sun. Too much light down here. It doesn't keep people healthy. It makes them act like fools."

*T*he police were gracious and extremely polite. I would have preferred them to be aggressive and mean and ready to treat any potential criminal like dogs. I hoped Jules would find Mathilde. I wanted to see them question her. Knowing she was a common thief would rid them of their manners.

"You were in Vence the other night?" they asked Sophie.

Sophie handed the younger police man the bottle and a white napkin. "Would you please do the honors?"

He moved away from the table and twisted the cork open.

She poured out the wine and gave us each a glass. I noticed that she had not answered the policeman's question, though there was no reason not to.

"Is there something wrong?"

"Yes," the policeman said as he sipped the wine. But I could have told her this.

"The candlesticks," I said.

Sophie shot me a look, but I couldn't help it. What was the use in pretending not to know what they were talking about?

Sophie asked us to explain. "I'm very confused," she said. She was straining to use her best flirting voice, but it wasn't quite working. It came off as whiny.

"You know all this Sophie," I said. "I told you about the missing candlesticks."

"It slipped my mind," Sophie said. "I think because I'm not sure what the missing jewelry has to do with us?"

"Candlesticks," the policeman corrected.

She pursed her lips. "The missing items. I'm not sure why you think any of us would know what happened to them."

The one assured her she had nothing to worry about. "Most likely it doesn't have a thing to do with you," he explained. "We're simply making inquiries to all who were there."

"There were a lot of people at the chapel that night," Sophie said.

They nodded. "We realize that," the one said. "The crowd there that night have made our lives extremely difficult."

She began talking very fast, explaining the night as if she had been there. She said she didn't think Grandfather had spent very much time in the chapel.

I shot her a look. These men were police. They were not men you lied to. Pretending to find a note from a drunk sailor in a bottle was one thing, but lying when they were investigating a robbery of two gold candlesticks was a criminal offense. I had to protect her from herself.

"She wasn't there," I said.

The policeman asked me what I meant.

"I mean my sister wasn't at the consecration ceremony that night."

The one closest to Sophie put down his wineglass. He wiped his mouth with the back of his hand and asked Sophie if what I said was true.

"I wasn't," Sophie said. "I meant to go, but in the end, I didn't."

"And yet you gave us the impression that you were there," they said.

"You told us there was a crowd. You were aware of the fact that your Grandfather spent most of the night in the gardens."

"My sister told me," Sophie said. "She was very excited to be there and we've talked often about that night."

We had discussed the night so I nodded. This was true.

"My Grandfather has bad eyes. He's almost blind. He suffers the same malady as Matisse. Isn't that amusing?"

I didn't think it was amusing. Neither did the police, but they liked the wine. Sophie refilled their glasses.

I didn't really think they thought Sophie was guilty, but she was acting oddly. She went around and passed the bowl of olives to the three men. One of them took a few. He popped them all into his mouth, then I watched as he put the pits in his pants' pockets.

I didn't realize there was a third policeman. We heard a knock at the front door, and then footsteps in the hall. He called out a tentative hello. Sophie got up and poked her head out the door.

"We're in here," she said.

The wine bottle was empty, but Sophie offered him some of the appetizers.

He refused.

"Who owns the black Cadillac?" he asked.

"Jules Agard," I said.

"And where is this Mr. Agard?"

Sophie laughed as if our domestic problems were funny. "It's a bit complicated."

"He's not here right now," I said.

"But his car is?"

"Yes," Sophie said.

I didn't see a reason to stall the inevitable. "Our maid ran away," I explained.

"Why?" he asked. "Is she in trouble? Has she done something wrong?"

"Yes," I said at the exact moment that Sophie was shaking her head no.

"Which is it?"

"She's done nothing wrong."

I had almost convinced myself that Mathilde was guilty of doing something wrong that I wanted to tell them the story of the stolen billfold, but Sophie held me back.

"She just ran away?" he asked. "Without reason?"

"She's an emotional girl. Mr. Agard has gone to look for her."

They exchanged glances. Sophie was too flustered and she was making everyone nervous.

"Let me explain," Sophie said. "I want a chance to explain everything."

"Jules didn't take them," I said. "He wouldn't. He told me he didn't."

Sophie told me to calm down. "I know what happened," she told the police.

"It looks like we do, too," the policeman said.

"It wasn't Jules," I repeated. "He wouldn't steal from Matisse."

"Give me the time to say something," Sophie said. She sent me upstairs. "Go," she hissed.

I was outraged, but she was adamant. "Help me, Agnes. Go upstairs. Don't make this worse."

"Don't let them arrest Jules," I pleaded.

"Let me take care of it," Sophie said.

Sophie was no match for the police. They would put Jules in jail and it would be years before I would see him again. I couldn't wait that long.

Sophie would hear none of my excuses. "If you do what I say, everything will be all right."

I went up the steps, like a child, though the rage inside me felt very adult.

I stood at the open window. The police were conferring with Sophie who, if nothing else, was talking too much. Jules stood beside her, his head bent. He didn't speak.

Several minutes later, Sophie and Jules got in his car. The police vehicle followed them out the gates, then both disappeared. I believed that Jules had taken the candlesticks, though he had said he hadn't. I knew he adored Matisse and that he had lied about that for the same reason he had lied to me about Normandy—he was ashamed.

I went downstairs and tiptoed into the kitchen. Mathilde didn't see me. She would not have spoken with such emotion, with such obvious abandon, if she had known I was listening.

"He was wonderful. Simply the most wonderful person in the whole world."

Cook was busy preparing a chicken for some dinner in the future. We were not eating that night. She plucked the feathers from its skin. She was quick and her wrists moved swiftly. "I find it hard to believe that anyone in this house is wonderful," she said.

"My knight in shining armor," Mathilde gushed. "He came to my rescue when I needed him."

I couldn't keep quiet. "You were hardly in dire straits," I said.

They turned to look, the chicken fell on the floor and Cook swore that she had had enough.

I was bold with Mathilde. "You stole money, then you ran away to the mountains in broad daylight."

"You are a horrible girl," Mathilde said. "You think I don't know what you're doing? I understand jealousy and that's what you are."

I turned away, my back against the stone wall.

"I was the one who loved your mother, who cared for her when no one in this house could stand to look at her."

"Shut up," I said.

"And you treat me like a dog," Mathilde said. "Like I don't have any feelings."

"Who cares about your feelings?" Jules was the one who was in trouble. He was the one who needed our help and all she could think about was herself.

"You think I'm nothing because I have no money," Mathilde said. Of course she didn't know what she was talking about. She never did. I hated her because she was from Normandy, because she had known Jules as a young boy, because it seemed as if he was interested in her. I hated her for treating me as if my feelings didn't matter. But she twisted everything into a different shape until I couldn't recognize it and didn't know how to fight it.

"You don't know what I think," I said. "You don't know me."

"I have hated this family since your mother died," Mathilde said. "She was the only one worth the work."

"Mathilde, stop," Cook demanded. "Don't say anymore. Everyone is upset. The house has turned for the worse. Let's just move forward. Everyone is safe. Everyone is in good health."

Mathilde was enraged and couldn't leave me alone. "You lie because you're green with jealousy."

"I am not jealous of you," I shouted. "I would never be jealous of someone like you."

"Get out," Cook spoke to me.

"It's my kitchen," I said.

"Go," Cook said. "Get."

"I don't have to," I yelled, but I didn't want to stay.

I ran outside all the way to the back of the garden where I found Grandfather crouching behind the garden shed.

"Are the police gone?" he asked.

"They've been gone for hours," I said.

He stood and thanked me for keeping an eye out for him. I had too much on my mind to think about his eccentric behavior. "Go back in the house," I said.

"But if you want my advice, I'd avoid the kitchen. They're crazy in there."

"I always do," he said, and then did as I told him.

The car headlights flashing on the wall alerted me to the fact that Sophie had returned. I got up and ran to the hallway. I pulled open the door to find Sophie searching for her key. It had never been locked.

The car that dropped her off was already leaving. From where I stood, I could not tell if it belonged to Jules or the police.

Mathilde came up behind me; she must have been waiting just as anxiously as I had been for Sophie's return.

I burned at her audacity.

"Is everything okay?" she directed the question to Sophie.

Sophie came into the house and once in the foyer she lit a cigarette and spoke with a gentle calm. "It is. Thank you, Mathilde. Jules is fine. It's late. He went home. He said he'd see you tomorrow."

"Thank you, Sophie," Mathilde said and went back down the hall. Her slippers shuffled on the tiles.

"Is that the truth?" I asked. "Is everything fine?"

"It is," Sophie said. She slumped into the chair and closed her eyes.

"What happened?"

"I'm too tired for explanations," Sophie said.

"You owe it to me," I said. "Jules didn't take the candlesticks," I said. "I know. I was with him all evening in Vence. I never once left his side."

"I know, *Cherie*," she said and stroked my cheek. "You're right."

"I am?"

"Yes," Sophie said. "Jules didn't take them."

This wasn't the answer I had been expecting. "Then how did they get in his car?"

"Someone put them there."

"But who would do that?" I asked. "Who would want to get Jules in trouble?" I thought of Mathilde, but couldn't see the sense in her having anything to do with the candlesticks.

"I don't think that was the point," Sophie said.

"But it happened," I said. "The police thought he was guilty. He could have spent the rest of his life in jail."

"I think they just wanted to make sure they weren't caught with them."

I waited for an explanation, but Sophie said we had something more important to do than talk about what had happened.

"Now?"

"I think it's for the best," she said.

Sophie went to the kitchen and found two working torches. Sophie began to search the house. She opened all drawers, looked in every cupboard, and lifted every rug.

"Will you at least tell me what we're looking for?" I asked.

"If I knew I would," she said. "But I don't."

"Will I know if I see it?"

"You will," she promised.

We moved through the house. In Grandfather's bottom drawer, in his bedroom, a room that hadn't been used in months, she found several china figurines.

"I thought so," she said.

She pulled open the drawer and took them out one by one. There were several of them. She lined them up on the dresser and we looked at them.

"Do you know anything about these?" she asked.

I fingered them carefully. "They're Hilda Koch's," I said remembering her distress that afternoon when she told me about her missing figurines.

Grandfather had wrapped them in an old gray blanket, the same kind that had hidden the candlesticks.

"Grandfather took these?"

"I'm afraid so," Sophie said.

They were very delicate. Animals with long noses, tiny boats, flowers with stems and petals. Brightly colored and miniature, they were hand painted with care.

"Grandfather covets things," Sophie said. "He takes things that aren't his."

"Did he take things in Paris?" I asked.

Sophie let out a laugh, but she wasn't having any fun. "He took a lot of things."

"From where?"

"Where didn't he take them from?" Sophie asked. She bent forward and let her hair hang over her head. She moaned as if in pain. "From department stores, from museums, from people's homes."

"You hid them from Father," I said. I remembered that night in our Paris bedroom when she had unwrapped something from around her waist. It must have been a print, something she had tried to hide from Father.

"As much as I could."

"And that's why we left Paris?" I asked. "Because of Grandfather?"

Sophie nodded.

"Was he in trouble with the police there?"

"Father did everything he could to keep him from getting arrested. The police sometimes called, though some of the owners took pity on him because he's an old man. Father pleaded and bargained and finally gave up."

"The scandal was Grandfather's fault," I said, finding it hard to believe that cantankerous, lazy Grandfather had that much power.

"One of the last things he took was a very expensive print from a small museum near the Sorbonne. I returned it, but the curator was furious and went directly to the police."

"How did he get it?"

"He's very good," Sophie said. "He came in with a sharp knife. He sat on a bench, complained of feeling faint. The guard went to get him a glass of water and while the room was empty, Grandfather cut the print from the frame."

"That's what he did the night in Vence."

"I should have been there," she said. "But I thought he'd respect a church."

"Grandfather doesn't care a thing about art," I mused.

"Not at all," Sophie said. "He probably doesn't even admire these miniature figures. He probably can't even see them that well."

"What are the police here going to do?" I asked.

"Nothing," she said. "I told them the truth. Grandfather's sick. He can't help himself."

"And they agreed not to press charges?"

"They're not going to put him in jail," Sophie said. "I begged them not to contact Father."

"Will they?"

"I don't think so," she said. "I offered to pay a fine. To give money to the chapel. They said they'd ask Matisse. Mostly they seemed relieved to have the candlesticks back."

She took out her cigarettes and lit one. She smoked for a minute, then stubbed it out on the leg of the dresser. The smoke hung low in the air.

I played with the figurines, each of them was so different than the other.

"We should return these," I said. "Hilda would want them back."

"Let's go now," Sophie said. She got up and started wrapping the figurines.

"Now?" I asked. "It's the middle of the night."

"I want to get this over with."

We walked to Hilda Koch's house. We used our torches, the small beams of light. The gate to her property was locked. I suggested we climb over, but Sophie thought this was going too far.

She had a large mailbox that was large enough for all of them to fit. Sophie took them out of her sack and set them carefully inside.

"Should we leave a note?" I asked.

"I think she'll know who they're from."

"She'll be furious."

"Then it doesn't matter if we leave a note," Sophie said.

"The important thing is that she's getting them back," I said.

"That's what I always say."

"It should make her happy to have them back."

"At least someone will be happy," Sophie said.

But I was, too. I was relived to know that Jules was innocent. Sophie was right—Grandfather was sick. He couldn't help himself. But Jules would have been a different story. He would have done it deliberately and for selfish reasons. I was very pleased that he was not the one to blame.

It was dawn by the time we made it back to Les Lianes. Sophie said she was exhausted. "I'm going to bed and I may never wake up."

I wasn't tired in the least. I stretched out on my bed and stared at the ceiling. I heard the hedgehogs that night. They were in the walls. They ran up and down burrowing about—their nails scratched on the wood as they played inside their cavernous homes.

*T*hough no one told me, I knew Jules and Mathilde were seeing each other. They tried to hide it from me, but I knew. I wasn't stupid. I knew when he came to get her. I knew when she went down the road to meet him. I knew they spent certain nights together. I knew when she rushed us through our evening meal.

I had always known about Jules' divided heart. When it came to things he was passionate about, he could not decide. Art vs. sport. Mathilde vs. Agnes. It was possible for him to give his attention to two things at the same time.

He was seeing Mathilde. Fine, I had to accept that. But in my favor was the first part of the summer. The enormous amount of time *we* had spent together. Just because he was entertaining Mathilde did not mean that he had forgotten about me.

Then the charade ended. And I discovered the reason why he had spent all those days with me.

Cook was the one who told me the truth.

I was in the kitchen watching Cook. With nothing to do with

my days, I suddenly got in everyone else's business. This was my day to pick on Cook.

Cook was always cutting things, but she was slow in making them into meals. She had cut vegetables all morning long, but the omelet or stew or whatever it was she had in mind for our dinner was not yet in the oven. She had a basket of fruit—peaches and apricots—and was in the process of cutting these as if she meant to bake a pie, but I doubted the pie would come to fruition by evening time. It wouldn't have surprised me if she didn't just cut, then toss all those small pieces in the garbage can. She was talking a blue streak about something. Talking about this, about that. I half listened, but poked around wondering what I could make myself to eat.

"That's what happens," Cook said. "Believe me. I've been in this situation a thousand times before. They always end up together."

"Is that right?" I asked. I was pleased to find an onion tart hidden under a dishtowel. It was not baked, but it was made.

"That's right," Cook said. She came over and took the tart from me. "Don't nibble the crusts. It looks like a mouse got to it."

"Who?" I asked.

"The hired help." She pressed her fingers together. "I could have predicted it."

"Hired help?" I asked. "Who are you talking about?"

"Those two," Cook said. "The pair of them."

"Who?" I asked again.

"That girl and your fancy car man," Cook said.

"Jules isn't hired," I said.

"Oh no?" she raised her eyebrows as if confused.

"Of course not," I said.

She grunted as if she was no longer interested in the conversation, but I had to set her straight. "No one pays him."

"You're so young," Cook said.

"What does that mean?" I asked. "What does my age have to do with anything?"

"This house should be renamed the house of too many secrets."

I had enough of her beating around the bush. If she wanted to tell me something she should tell me. I didn't want a guessing game every time I came into the kitchen.

I grabbed the knife from her hand and threw it across the room. "Stop," I commanded. "Tell me what you're talking about."

"You've lost your mind," she said. She clicked her fingers. "Pick that up. Pick that up now. Only a fool throws things like that."

I was a fool.

"If you have something to tell me, then tell me. If not, then shut your mouth." I waited but she said nothing. I walked up next to her. She turned to face me. I walked right into her. She resisted with her arms folded across her chest.

"You're an evil girl," Cook hissed at me. "You'll come to no good with this kind of behavior."

I was bold. I was evil. I was everything she thought about me. I pushed her with my hands. She thought it was a mistake and backed away from me But I came at her. I walked into her, pushing her with my shoulders and my anger.

"Ask your sister if she didn't pay that man," Cook said. "And if she tells you no, she's lying. I saw it with my own eyes."

"You're the one who lies," I said, and shoved all my weight against her. I had blocked her into the corner; she didn't have too far to fall.

The scene was made worse by Cook's screaming that I was a lunatic.

I searched the villa for Sophie. I found her in Grandfather's study. She was asleep on the sofa, a book opened on her lap. I stormed in and confronted her with all my anger of the last few weeks.

"You paid him," I said.

She woke immediately and sat up. "I haven't the slightest idea what you're talking about."

"You paid Jules to be my friend," I shouted.

"You're not in one of your frantic moods again, are you?" Sophie asked. "I've spent every ounce of energy trying to make you happy this summer. I was so sure it was working." The pattern of the sofa had made an imprint on her cheek.

"Tell me the truth," I said.

"What truth?" she asked. "What is it that you want to know?" Her hair had come undone and she twisted it back into a bun and fastened the barrette to hold it in place at the base of her neck.

"Did you give Jules money?" I yelled at her.

"This whole scene seems dramatic and unnecessary," Sophie said.

"I'm not interested in your opinion. I want to know the truth. Yes or no?"

"Yes," she said quickly. "I did. I gave him money."

"To babysit me? You paid him to take care of me, as if he was my nanny?"

"I wouldn't use those terms to explain your situation, but in answer to the other question, yes. I gave him money."

"Why?"

"Because he needed it."

I fell to the floor and put my forehead against the tiles.

"That's the problem with not having a job. Money doesn't grow on trees."

"He was my babysitter. You paid him to take care of me."

"Why are you so crazy?"

"You don't understand," I cried.

"Agnes, I don't know anyone who wouldn't envy your life. You've had a lovely time these past weeks. Why ruin it with all this unnecessary emotion? I gave him money because he needed it."

"It's not fair."

"Stop it. You're like a four-year-old throwing a tantrum. What's wrong? Tell me." She knelt beside me and put her arms around me.

The tears burst forth. "I love him."

The whole thing had been a sham.

"Oh, sweetheart," she said. "Don't cry."

"Why? What does it matter?" I had nothing to live for. No reason to get up. I would die, or spend the rest of my life looking at the black and ivory tiles. I would never leave the room. I would stop eating. I would stop breathing and then one day, weighing nothing, I would just float to my death.

"Don't do this," Sophie said.

"Why not?"

"But why are you acting like this?" she said.

"Because he never loved me. I thought he did."

"How do you know he doesn't?"

"He came to the house every day because you paid him."

"Maybe he did both," Sophie said.

I stopped crying. She was offering me a ray of hope with these words. I listened. I urged her to continue.

"For all I know he might be terribly in love with you. And broke. They're not mutually exclusive. Lots of poor people are in love."

I had a reason to lift my head, so I did. "Do you really think that?"

"I don't know, sweetie, I just don't know. "

"But do you think it could be true."

"I don't mean to offer you false hope, but there's always the possibility that it could be true."

"Help me," I pleaded. I was an explorer trapped in a dark tunnel. Suddenly a shaft of light had flashed up ahead. I wanted to be taken to the light.

*T*rue to her word, Sophie got in touch with Jules the next day and asked if he could come up to the villa. She had something she wanted to discuss with him.

He came right away.

"*Darling*," Sophie got up from the chair. "Come here for a moment, if you have time."

"*Darling*," Jules said. "What a pleasant surprise. Of course I have time for you. When don't I have time for you?"

They kissed. She offered him a cigarette. He accepted. The chair he sat in was wet from the morning dew.

I had everything to lose or gain by their conversation and though Sophie told me specifically that she did not want me to be about, I went inside the house but stood on the other side of the door. The windows were open.

She wasted no time getting to the point. "My sister is in love with you."

Jules danced about, hands in his pockets. He seemed happy and pleased with himself, which gave me hope, the last moment of hope I had that morning.

"Who wouldn't be in love with me?" Jules joked.

Sophie laughed. It was hard to watch—two of them laughing and joking in the bright sunshine—I wanted to rush out and tell them to be serious. This was my life they were discussing.

"Did you know that?"

"I haven't done anything wrong, Sophie," Jules said.

"Oh, Jules, I'm not suggesting you did. I'm just telling you what Agnes told me."

"I haven't done anything disrespectful."

"Oh, god, Jules, don't get defensive," Sophie said. "I'm not accusing you of anything."

"It certainly sounds like you are."

"Not in any way," Sophie said. She finished her cigarette; the gray-white smoke circled her head. "I'm just asking. You spent the summer with her—maybe something developed. I haven't actually been keeping great track of Agnes these past weeks. I'm a bit consumed with my own affair of the heart."

"I told you nothing went on between us. I did exactly as you asked me to. I entertained her."

"I trust you, Jules. I'm asking you because she's young and probably has misunderstood your attention."

"She had fun. I had fun. You had time to be with the good doctor. It seemed to have worked out for the best, darling."

"It did. It did. But now she's in love with you. I'm simply asking if you're in love with her."

"She's a kid."

"But she's not a baby," Sophie said. "She has feelings."

I had heard enough. I got up and walked away from the house. The garden was overgrown and the tall weeds and flowers scratched my legs, but I walked to the edge of the property.

I don't know if Sophie encouraged Jules to follow me or if he did it on his own.

"Stop, Agnes," he called. "Wait. I want to talk to you."

The heat in the garden was intense. The sun directly overhead, it burned into my head.

"What do you want?" I hissed like a mad cat.

"Don't be angry," he said. "I never meant to make you angry."

I called him a traitor. "I know of no worse crime than treason."

"How can you call me that? What did I do?"

"You betrayed everyone."

"I never made any romantic advances," Jules said. "I never misled you."

He had no guilt, no remorse. I couldn't live knowing he felt nothing for our summer together.

"I'm not talking about me," I said.

I attacked him where I thought it might do the most damage. "You said you adored Coppi. You stood on the top of the mountains and made me swear that I adored him too."

He smiled. I saw it and his ease and attitude with the situation infuriated me further. "Admit it. We had fun this summer. What's wrong with that?"

"Having fun?" I asked. "Nothing is wrong with it. I'm not against fun."

"Well, then," he said. Hand back in his pocket, he had finished talking with me. He wasn't harmed by the afternoons spent with me. He had his money. Everything else was a game. He had done his duty and now it was time to move. I was the loser. I had misunderstood the rules and now was alone, my heart broken into millions of pieces of hurt and anger. No one cared. No one cared, but me.

The nettles were sharp and bit my legs. I tried to push forward.

"I'm sorry you misunderstood my intentions."

I had been a fool, but I still had the fight in me. "For all I know, you don't even like Matisse. You probably don't care at all about Coppi."

"I never lied to you about those things."

"You lied to me about everything else."

Jules held up his hand like he was taking an oath. "Believe this, Agnes, if you believe anything. I tell stories. I do. But the truth is that Coppi and Matisse are great men. They would never lie. They would never have hurt you like I did. But I'm not like them. I'm not even close."

"You are not even the lanterne rouge."

"I'm not even in the race."

Jules didn't love me. For all I knew, he didn't even like me.

I walked away.

I was miserable but rather than wallow in it, I simply pretended that nothing was wrong. Jules was gone. But the Riviera was not. I didn't need him. I was fifteen years old. I continually reminded myself that I was a person who lived in the present. I had my future ahead of me.

Les Lianes was quieter. The halls seemed to echo more. The position of the sun was changing. Night came earlier and stayed longer.

I was stubborn. I was not going to give Jules that much power. He was a short little man with not much more than admiration in his head and without Sophie footing the bills, he had nothing in his pockets. If he didn't find me attractive, I wasn't going to waste my pining after him. I had to simplify it. I swallowed my anger and when Sophie asked if I was okay, I held up my chin and spoke in a loud monotone. "Why shouldn't I be okay?"

"Do you miss Jules?"

"He was a liar," I said. "I don't miss people who lie to me. I don't want to be around people who hide from the truth."

Sophie frowned and tried to press the issue. "I worry about you."

My bones felt brittle. I really thought that one day I would simply walk into the sea and continue to the horizon. I would never turn back. I would just walk on and on until the ocean waters covered me completely.

Fausto Coppi had a terrible Tour de France. I sat in the study with Grandfather and listened to the reports of the daily stages. Coppi started out fine. He wasn't in the top spot, but he wasn't too far behind.

"He's a climber," Grandfather informed me.

"The Tour is decided in the mountain stages," I said.

Grandfather, not used to having anyone engaged in the things that interested him, was competitive with me. "Sprinters never win."

"Coppi is no sprinter," I countered back.

"He's one of the greatest cyclists Italy has ever produced."

Grandfather was wasting his breath telling me facts about Coppi. I knew every detail. I had a hard time walking downstairs in the morning and I marveled at how Coppi could race every day. I'm sure his heart was heavy with sadness after his brother's death, and I wept for him.

Grandfather's eyes, getting worse almost every day, gave me the privacy I wanted and I could cry openly without questions or concerns.

After three weeks and 4,690 kilometers, Coppi rode into Paris in 10th place, forty-six minutes behind Hugo Koblet. He was interviewed for a few moments; everyone agreed that it was one of his worst races.

"Give him a break," I yelled at the radio.

"The public cares only about those who win," Grandfather informed me and I told him truer words had never been spoken.

"The world cares nothing for losers."

"As it should be," Grandfather said.

But I disagreed. I believed in loyalty. I believed in love.

One afternoon, bored and tired of doing nothing but argue with Grandfather, I took the bus to Villefranche-sur-Mer. An antique market filled the plaza by the sea. I walked from booth to booth admiring the pieces. There were too many candlesticks.

I walked along the boardwalk. It was warm and the beaches were filled with bathers. Groups of kids my age were there in groups of five or six. I had never noticed them before. I bought an ice cream. I watched them, but grew tired of their laughter.

I turned back towards town. I wanted to go home. I had been there less than an hour. Maybe the next day would be better. My heart hurt as I walked along the quay, squinting into the sun.

That's when I saw Richard. He was at a table in the restaurant, the last one on the boardwalk, the one with the bright yellow umbrellas, the tablecloths, and silverware. The restaurant where the waiters wore short black jackets, long white aprons, and ties. The one I had never been to because we could not, as Jules said, even afford to look at the menu.

Richard was not alone. He sat with a woman and two children. They were dressed for a Sunday lunch. The woman and the girl wore matching hair ribbons. I watched them eat their meal.

I didn't have to be told that it was his wife and children; their attitude made this apparent. I stood a few feet away. The woman noticed me, but she avoided my gaze. When they were done, I followed them down the boardwalk. I walked directly behind the little boy, right on his heels. I was too close for him to avoid me. The boy was too shy to say anything. He tried to walk faster. I did too. He was confused by my close presence, but finally understood that I was doing this on purpose. He said something to his mother.

She turned her head and stared at me. I stared back.

The woman told Richard about me. "That girl is following us," she said. "She watched us the whole time we were eating."

Richard mumbled something. The wind was always stronger the closer you got to the shoreline, and I couldn't hear him.

"She doesn't look like she wants money," the woman said.

If Richard had any worries or concerns about seeing me, he did not show it. He gave me his big smile, one I did not return.

"Agnes," he said. "How are you? How is your grandfather? How is his eyesight? Still a concern?"

He had nerve. I was shocked at his ease, the way he could pretend that all this was normal. I lowered my eyes into little slits and hissed at him like I was a poisonous snake.

I hissed louder, the children laughed, but then when I did not speak, they ran to hide behind their mother's skirt.

The woman asked me if everything was all right. "Can she speak?" she asked Richard.

"Give my best to your Grandfather," Richard said. His smile was huge, all white teeth and dark moustache.

I was appalled at his ease.

"My grandfather's almost blind," I shouted. "Maybe if he had had a real doctor, one who could really help him, one who takes time with his patients, instead of wasting days in the neighboring cafés, he might be able to see today."

Richard asked if I was feeling all right.

His wife pulled on his shirtsleeve. "Let's go," she pleaded.

"Of course I'm not feeling all right. But what does it matter to you? What do any of our feelings matter to you?"

Richard hushed me. "There's no reason for a scene," he directed. "If your Grandfather needs attention, I'd be happy to see him."

"And the rest of us?" I screamed. "Do you have time for all of us?"

People had stopped and were watching my show.

"It's a strange family," I heard Richard tell his wife.

"At least none of us are married," I yelled.

Disgusted with the world, myself included, I trudged over to the center of town and waited for a bus. One finally came. It was jammed with a happy Sunday crowd. I went to the back and took a seat with no window and no view. The last thing I wanted to see was the Mediterranean. The sun was too bright and I did not want to watch the colors of light dancing across the water.

*S*ophie was on the patio with a book and her cigarettes. I stood in the doorway, watching her. She wasn't happy. I saw her fidget. But when she saw me standing there, she pretended that everything was okay.

"How was the beach?" she asked.

"It was there," I said.

"It usually is," she said. She looked up and I met her gaze.

"I saw Richard," I said.

"Oh?" She put her head in her book and turned the page as if the words before her were more interesting than my discovery that Richard had a wife and children.

"Have you seen him lately?" I had been so consumed by my own affairs of the heart that I had forgotten about Sophie.

"He's been very busy," she said. "It's not easy with the practice and everything."

Sophie lit her cigarette, a movement that showed her nonchalance as if we were discussing the change of weather.

"He wasn't alone," I said.

She nodded and then she spoke wistfully. "No. I don't imagine he'd be at the beach alone on a nice Sunday afternoon." She was tired of hiding things, tired of holding everything in.

"How long have you known?" I asked.

She sighed and smoked, but did not answer.

"You do know, don't you?" I didn't think we had to spell it out for each other. We were two grown women who had lost much in love.

"Yes," she said. "I know about his wife and children. He has a little girl and a little boy. Ages six and four respectively. I know all about them. I know less about his wife, since I ask fewer questions about her, he doesn't tell me as much."

She was bitter, her voice full of quiet rage, which was in such contrast to her joy of only a few weeks ago.

"Close your mouth," Sophie instructed. "Flies will buzz in and you'll swallow them and die."

"It's not true," I said.

"It's not," she said. "Your teeth are too big. The flies would never get in and if they did, they'd get stuck trying to get out."

"It can't be true," I said. I slid off my chair and sat on the bricks, not caring that the dead palm leaves scratched at my bare legs. "This is intolerable. I can't bear it," I whispered. My unhappiness was overwhelming, but it was mine. I didn't want Sophie suffering the same disappointments.

"You do have a flair for the dramatic."

Romantic, handsome, funny Richard—with a wife and two ugly children? It wasn't possible. He was supposed to have been perfect.

"How can you be so flippant?" I yelled. "I saw you. You loved him. I thought you were going to be married this fall. Isn't your heart broken?"

"You don't have to yell. Many men have wives," Sophie said. "It's not like he has two heads."

"But not that you're in love with," I said. "I thought he was special."

She tried to flick her cigarette into the garden, but she didn't have the end grasped the right way and it fell at her feet.

"It does make it more complicated than I wanted it to be, but I've gotten used to it."

"You knew he was inappropriate when you met him?"

"I guessed from the start."

"But you didn't know?"

"Not right away," she said.

"When then?" I asked. "When did he tell you that he was married?"

"He told me the truth when I asked. He never lied."

I shook with rage at my sister's humiliation.

"That's something," Sophie said. "Believe me. Many men would have tried to keep it from me."

"Why aren't you more upset?"

Sophie shrugged, then started to say something. The muscles in her jaw twitched. She put her hand up to her face and covered her eyes. She started to protest, but the futility of trying to hide her emotions overtook her. Her face twisted in pain and I realized the depth of her sadness. She sobbed. There were no words, just deep breaths of despair. I went over to her chair and sat beside her. I held her and the two of us cried out our broken hearts.

What she said when she could finally speak was simple. "I want to go home," she said.

I knew what she meant; she was talking about Paris.

"I had such hopes when we first came down here," she said. "I thought this place was going to be magical. All the sun, the beautiful mountains, the sea right out our doorsteps. How could things not be different? How could they not be better?"

She had once been uncharacteristically optimistic; all that was gone now.

"I thought it best that we get Grandfather away from Father," Sophie said. "Without their constant fighting, I thought they might actually start to get along. As long as Father didn't see Grandfather, he wouldn't be bothered if Grandfather got out of hand every once in a while."

I knew what she meant.

"It just didn't work out the way I wanted."

"Nothing worked out." I agreed with her.

"I miss Mamma," she said. "Oh I wish she was here with us."

"Me too," I said, the first time I had ever admitted the desire I had for my mother.

We sat in the grove of bare citrus trees and cried. A few minutes later, Cook came out with a tray. She didn't ask why we were crying; she simply sat in the chair on the other end of the table and heaved her chest, a long sigh, as if she was just worn out. Sophie poured out some rosé wine for all three of us and we sipped that, but left the plates untouched. No one had an appetite. Grandfather wandered by a few times. He poured himself a glass of wine and took some pâté and spread it on a chunk of bread. "I'm assuming this is dinner," he said. No one replied. What was the point?

The storm caught us by surprise. The rain and winds rushed down the mountains without warning. We ran inside to take cover, leaving the tray on the patio table. Sometime during the night something knocked it over—a hedgehog, a bird, or maybe the wind. The broken bits of kitchenware scattered across the bricks where we left them. Unless the new owners swept them away, they are there still.

Chapter Ten

I wanted Jules back. By some miracle of fate, I hoped that he would realize his loss, that he would miss me, that he would return—that one day, I would hear his tires on the gravel. He would come into the villa and beg my forgiveness. I imagined him declaring his love and I would forgive him for the awful way he had treated me. He was my destiny. We were witnesses of greatness and glory and we were fated to be together.

But he never came.

One day we were driving in his black Cadillac chasing after Coppi, trying to catch a glimpse of Matisse and the next he was gone. Vanished from my life forever.

And though I wanted to, I never saw him again.

I heard from Cook that he and Mathilde married and moved north to Normandy. If that were true, then I imagined him to be a ruined man. A man who had lost his reason for living. For what did he have without the sun, the dazzle, and the warm leisure of the Côte d'Azur? Furthermore, what did his unhappiness have to do with me? We were not related, not quite peers, there was nothing to connect us or to keep us in touch with each other. What we shared was over.

Mathilde's trousseau was sent for. Sophie paid. "I'm not sure why I'm responsible for this," she said, but her heart was not really into the complaint. I did not have the heart to inquire where she was shipping it. She did not tell me.

Grandfather refused the eye operation and his sight grew worse. His paranoia increased and he became dreadful, not just bothersome, but impossible to live with.

After many requests, and much pleading, Father came down.

In late September, the weather had changed dramatically. It rained every afternoon, the winds increasing with each passing day. With the drafts and gray skies, the villa was cold and gloomy. The vines had taken over the property. Thick and twisted, they seemed sinister in the way that they blocked the paths and climbed the garden walls.

Father was disappointed. "It used to be so beautiful," he said.

"It could be," Sophie said. "But it isn't. It's too much work."

He thought the place old and decrepit. We closed the house and then decided that it would be best to sell it. "Let someone else make it beautiful again," Father said. Had Sophie or I protested that we wanted to keep it in the family, I think he would have agreed. We didn't.

We packed quickly, leaving many of our things. "One would think you didn't have any fun here," Father said. "Though I've heard it's become quite the fashionable place to summer."

"It was fine," Sophie said, but we were both anxious to leave.

"Grandfather behaved himself?"

"He can't see," Sophie said. "What harm could he do?"

With this news, Father was quite pleased. His idea that time away from Paris, from the usual distractions, had worked.

*P*aris was just as we had left it. After a few weeks, it was hard to remember that we had ever been gone. Our routines became our lives. I didn't forget my sadness, but I became occupied with other things. I was a year behind in my studies and had so much work to do to catch up with the other students in my level. They were surprisingly helpful and even anxious to be friends. I was someone who had done something different—my year on the Riviera made me curious and people were anxious to talk to me. I enjoyed my sudden turn of popularity. I worked hard. I studied and sat for my exams. I was not brilliant, but I did better than I thought I would.

I turned eighteen.

I didn't forget about our time in the Riviera, but I didn't like thinking of it. I was embarrassed by my naïveté. I was ashamed of my youth and thought myself foolish for falling so much in love. I was horrified at how I had treated Mathilde. Especially because of my mother. My mother had loved her and I had been a brat. I did my best to think of other things.

Sophie spent a great deal of time that year with my mother's relatives in Belgium. There she fell madly in love with a distant cousin of my mother's.

I lived in the apartment with my father and my grandfather, an arrangement I learned to like. I liked our formal dinners, our depen-dence on conversation, almost as if we were afraid to have silence because silence would have been trouble. We talked most often about France and her troubles, though we occasionally considered the rest of the world.

I passed my baccalaureate, which made my father very proud. I was following the traditions of France before all had been lost.

I hung out with my friends until early morning. I came home, I slept most of the day, woke in the afternoon, drank coffee, brooded about, went to the market, bought dinner for the three of us, went home, cooked. By the time dinner was ready, the lamps would be lit. We would have coffee and listen to music. My father would offer to clean up. "I'm fine," I'd say. "I don't mind."

I would bring in a brandy and drink while I did the washing up.

Later, after both of them had retired to their rooms, I would leave and the cycle would start again. I liked the repetition of my days. I liked knowing what would come next and the general ease I had at doing nothing. I rarely thought about the future.

My father was convinced Sophie was about to marry. I knew differently.

Sophie told me the man she was seeing was a bit inappropriate, so I guessed he was married.

My father would like to move to Denmark. I think he wants to rid himself of France and the misery of the country's memories. I ask him to wait—at least until we know what is happening with Sophie.

"I can help plan her wedding from Copenhagen."

"Perhaps you should learn the language before you move to a new country," I advise. "It might be useful to be able to communicate with the people there."

I never want to leave France. I never want to see the world.

We live in a quiet neighborhood near the Basilica. Grandfather is still the same, though this doesn't offer me any comfort. Our apartment is on the seventh floor and the elevator, a charming glass structure where one can see the pulleys and wires, is always breaking down. My father would like to see a new one installed, but I organized the tenants and we protested to keep the old one. A new elevator would ruin the integrity of the building. Moreover, it isn't necessary.

"But a new one would be extremely efficient," my father argues. "It wouldn't break down every other morning."

"There's nothing wrong with a little inefficiency," I tell him. "We don't need perfection."

This is part of my caution. I prefer things the way they are.

"Fine," he says, but he refuses to hear my complaints when the elevator gets stuck on the fourth floor and I am forced to carry the groceries up the stairs.

I am generally opposed to speed—especially when it comes to travel. I see no reason for so much air travel—where is the luxury of a clock that doesn't run on time?

I am pleased to hear that the engineers developing the super-fast trains are running into problems. It seems that the vibration on the rails will affect the vineyards and crops of the countryside. They have to find a way not to disturb the earth as they race past.

"They will find a way to perfect them," my father predicts with assurance.

In the meantime, there are still boats and regular trains that move quickly enough for me. I am the only person in the world who does not care about space travel. I could not care if the Americans or the Russians or the British land a spaceship on the moon. The world is big enough for all of us. Why waste good money trying to get to uninhabitable, inhospitable places?

My father accuses me of romancing the past.

"Is that what it is?" I ask. I'm not so sure; I dread change because I think it means loss. My experiences have taught me this and I believe in my own life.

This past year the Paris transit authorities changed the color of the Metro tickets. It was a decision entirely without reason. The tickets had always been yellow. For years. When I think of Paris, I think of thousands of yellow metro tickets strewn in the gutters, on the sidewalks, everywhere. Decades of yellow, then suddenly they decided the tickets would be green. The streets look cheap with the scattered pieces of chartreuse. I went to every window and asked for a *carnet* of yellow tickets and was informed that the entire system was now green. Only green.

My father was amused by my letter to *Le Figaro*, the one I wrote in protest of these senseless actions. I wrote in support of the French who cared about tradition, who didn't need change, who didn't want everything to be different every time they walked down the street. My husband thought it was touching. "Your words touched a chord with people. Their hearts are with yours."

When I read my letter—printed with the small headline—"Angry Parisian Challenges Color Change"—I felt like I had won something.

"Victory is mine," I told my father.

He smiled and said that at least they had spelled my name right. There were no grammatical errors in my letter. "Your letter is quaint, but it hasn't done anything."

I thought he was wrong.

"It hasn't convinced them to change back."

"It's not the point," I explained.

"Then why write a letter of protest?"

"To let them know the past doesn't always have to be erased. Not without reason. New isn't always better."

"It isn't always worse."

I know I am not alone in wanting to preserve the past. I can walk down any street in Paris and see the centuries-old buildings, the bridges from Roman times. The design of the streets is Napoleonic and the gray slate roofs have been there forever. The city gives me great comfort. I identify with Paris.

*I*t had been nine years since I saw Fausto Coppi race in the Italian mountains. I heard his name often; he continued to race, he continued to win. Then I heard that he was hurt, that he was getting older, that he was having troubles racing. But whenever my husband or his friends talked sports, I would say Coppi's name and everyone always agreed—he was the greatest, one of the most admired athletes of his time.

A cold January morning and I was listening to the radio when I heard the news: Fausto Coppi was dead.

Forty years old, his death was a mistake. He had been on safari in Africa and had probably been bitten by a mosquito. The Italian doctor misdiagnosed his symptoms as flu and had done nothing for the malaria's fever.

Nine years had passed since that afternoon near San Remo. Besides the race in the Italian mountainside village, I had never watched another bicycle race, not even the Tour de France, which finishes in Paris every July.

Fausto Coppi would race no more. Fausto Coppi would breathe

no more. The tifosi grieved frantically. They were stunned and out-raged and demanded justice. The greatest racer in the world was dead. How could it have happened? He was betrayed by a misdi-agnosis. The flags of Italy flew at half-mast with everyone agreeing that he should have lived. Some things were meant to be. Not this. Oh no. This was a mistake.

Fifty thousand people crowded the streets of Castellania, Coppi's hometown. The burial was on the side of a mountain. The snow and fallow fields were like a giant chessboard of black and white squares. Just as mobs of people had come out over the years to watch him ride his bicycle, mobs came out to bury him. The hillsides were covered with people and cars, everyone pressing to get close to Coppi. His adoring fans were stunned; most of all, they were devastated.

The newspapers were filled of photographs and stories of his glo-rious achievements, his crushing tragedies. Later that day, I walked to the corner *tabac* to see how other countries were reporting his death.

The headline in the Italian sporting news reached for poetry to comfort the tifosi: "The great heron has closed his wings."

I put down my francs and the foreign man behind the counter picked them up without acknowledging me. But I had to tell someone.

"I knew him," I said, turning the paper so he could see the reason for my red eyes. The black headlines were bold. They ached with sadness and shock. Fausto Coppi is dead. The greatest will race no more.

He glanced at the newspaper, but made no comment.

I continued. "Once upon a time, I knew him."

I was being foolish, but couldn't help myself. I was crying. In public. I tried to justify it—a man had just died. I had every reason to cry, but I was overwhelmed with sentiments I thought I had buried long ago.

I cried not for Coppi, but for Jules. And for me—for my fifteen-year-old bold, enthusiastic, fearless self. I cried for the girl I had been.

I still missed Jules. I missed the way that we had spent our days. I missed the views of the Mediterranean. I missed the wind, the smell of lemons and jasmine. I missed the musty dank smell of Les Lianes. I missed my sister, not the Sophie of today, but the Sophie of yesterday—the young girl with her head in the *Nice-Matin* waiting on the incoming flights—the planes filled with eligible young men.

The man behind the counter did not care about my distress. At fifteen, I would have made fun of my behavior in the tabac that day, but it was suddenly important that he knew that I had been young once. I'm sure to him, I was just another crazy Parisian, mumbling about old times, of having once been in the presence of greatness.

My heart had never been divided. I had loved—recklessly, boundlessly, passionately. That it had not been returned was nothing to be ashamed of.

The shop was busy and the man asked me to move along so he could attend to the line of customers behind me.

I walked out into the rain, clutching the newspapers to my chest for warmth, not unlike the cyclists who pad their shirts at the top of the mountain passes so they will not freeze on the fast descents.

I know my time spent on the Riviera was not all glorious, but I do not recall the dismal moments in memory. I remember only the light and the way the sun shimmered across the endless sea.

For *The Long White*
"Sharon Dilworth's writing is animated and sympathetic, wry and aware. Her characters are vivid and unpredictable. She is able to convey a sense of life lived in time and place with great immediacy. The reader senses a complete world in the control of the author's sensibility; it is this, I think, that establishes the excellence of her work."

ROBERT STONE

For *Women Drinking Benedictine*
"Though Rubik's Cubes are no longer a national obsession, those colorful puzzles may keep coming to mind as you're reading Sharon Dilworth's second short-story collection, *Women Drinking Benedictine*. Her fiction is just as intricate: whenever one person moves, another is dislodged, and the pattern of the narrative grows more elaborate with each turn. But while someone struggling with a Rubik's Cube tries to twist everything back into alignment, Dilworth delights in doing the opposite. Characters initially arranged along familiar axes—husband and wife, mother and daughter, boyfriend and girlfriend—soon find themselves on unfamiliar ground."

LIAM CALLANAN, *The New York Times*

For *Year of the Ginkgo*
"Displaying the deadpan wit and psychological resonance that have long characterized her award-winning stories, Sharon Dilworth's debut novel traverses an exuberant journey along a wide range of emotions. Hilarious yet heartbreaking, darkly cynical yet surprisingly tender, *Year of the Ginkgo* explores the hidden intricacies of the American family with the profoundness and wisdom of *The Ice Storm* and *We Don't Live Here Anymore*. With characters and insights that linger long after being read, Dilworth deftly clears a compelling and delicate path from dissatisfaction to obsession to awareness to fulfillment, all the while progressing through themes as broad as marriage, infidelity, friendship and—perhaps most importantly—if you've ever wondered what secrets lurk behind the white picket fence, look no further than this book."

KEVIN GONZÁLEZ